Loving the Billionaire Ever After

Billionaire Brothers Series

Book 7

M.G. MORGAN

Loving the Billionaire Ever After
Copyright © 2014 M.G. Morgan
All Rights Reserved.

Chapter One

*S**WEAT RAN DOWN BETWEEN AARON'S shoulder blades as he crept forward. His field of vision was practically nil, the darkness surrounding them was strangely complete and unlike normal darkness. It was the first clue Aaron had that told him he was dreaming and he clung to it like a drowning man.*

The last place Aaron ever wanted to find himself again was back in the field surrounded by the other men of his group. Men that he would have trusted with his life…

Hank darted out ahead, the tactical rifle he held in his hands armed and ready for use. Aaron glanced down at his own assault rifle willing his body to lift it and fire off the rounds into Hank's back but his body refused to comply. He was dreaming and although he knew what was going on he wasn't in charge of what happened.

Hank disappeared around the side of one of the dilapidated warehouses and was gone from sight.

Aaron shuffled forward, his body moving automatically as they were given the all clear to advance. He wanted to shut his eyes, to hide from what was coming next but it was impossible. Aaron remembered this night, every little detail painfully etched into the inside of his head like a tattoo.

Why was it always this dream? Why was it always the memory of this night that plagued him?

He knew the answers to the questions but it didn't make it any easier. It was this night that had made his choice to leave easy. His doubts had suddenly become very solid reasons and he had handed in his resignation.

Gunfire ripped through the too black night and inside Aaron found himself cringing. He ran across the uneven ground his feet barely making noise as he positioned himself behind the door.

Screaming from inside the stone building gave Aaron all the encouragement he needed and without thinking he breached the door. The moment he was inside his training kicked in and carried him through the building.

There was a man sitting behind a table, his head slumped over onto his chest, dark liquid dripping slowly down onto the floor from the hole in the back of his head. Aaron swore silently under his breath and continued forward.

They had been given very strict instructions, the people inside were to be taken alive, whoever had beaten him into the building hadn't paid any heed to their orders.

There was blood smeared along the walls in the hall as though someone had been pressed up against the wall and dragged along its length. Aaron found the second body, the dead man's face still a mask of surprise as he lay in a dark puddle.

A gurgling sound caught Aaron's ear and he stepped over the body, his gun held ready. More sounds were carried to his ears and Aaron found himself unable to make out what the sounds were or what they meant. Or at least the Aaron who held the gun felt that way. Dream Aaron knew exactly what he was hearing. It had taken him a long time to figure it out.

Each time he had the dream it always cut off but the memories were still there. Perhaps it was his brain's way of trying to protect him, an attempt to seal him off from the responsibility he felt. A responsibility he should have felt more.

So many regrets...

Aaron froze with his hand on the door. There was no more noise, it had all dropped away into silence and he couldn't decide if that was good or bad.

He paused waiting for Paul to come in behind him, waiting for Paul to call to him and ask him what the hell had happened. Aaron would turn and shrug and then the door Aaron had just walked away from would swing open, Hank framed in the doorway, his dark clothes covered in black wet patches.

Paul didn't come and Aaron suddenly realised that he was back in control of the dream. It was no longer simply a recollection of a memory.

His body was suddenly overwhelmed with the smells in the room and Aaron fought the urge to gag. Gripping the door knob he twisted it hard, letting the door swing inwards.

The yellow swinging over head light cast an odd glow on the gruesome scene unfolding before him. Vomit fought its way up

3

Aaron's throat as he saw Hank in the centre of the room, the blade held high in his hand.

Aaron sprang upright in the bed, sweat causing the sheets to stick to him as he fought for air. The smells from the dream followed him and Aaron stumbled from the bed in an attempt to reach the bathroom.

He reached the toilet seconds before he spilled his guts into the bowl. His entire body was covered in a fine sheen of sweat and the cool air from the bathroom made him shiver.

Dropping back onto the floor, Aaron pressed his back against the wide bath. He closed his eyes and fought to calm his breathing, to bring it back down to a more manageable pace, or at least one where he didn't feel as though he might pass out.

The dream was different and new and Aaron knew exactly why he was having it now. He was responsible. He knew what Hank was, he knew he was a monster and yet he had invited him back into his life. It was Aaron's fault that Hank had chosen Kirsty, his fault that he had even met her.

Aaron pressed his hands hard against his face almost as though he could force the feelings of guilt and regret back inside. Push them so far down in his body that he wouldn't be forced to suffer with them every moment of the day.

Part of him wanted to argue that he didn't have a choice. That he had known what Hank was and had allowed him access to Kirsty. If it was a choice between his secretary or the woman he adored then there really couldn't be a choice.

Of course Aaron knew Heather wouldn't see it that way and that was one of the reasons she could never know the truth. If she found out that he knew what Hank was…

It just wasn't a risk he could take. Curling his hands into fists, Aaron beat them against the front of his head but it didn't do anything to help him shift the images from his dream. They had joined the other images he had seared in there and it was becoming harder and harder to decide which were memories and which he had created himself.

He shuddered violently and then paused.

He'd almost missed it, the sound of his own thoughts too loud as they stole his concentration. Aaron pushed his body upright, pressing his body up onto the balls of his feet as he crept from the bathroom and out into the bedroom.

The sound caught his attention again and this time there really was no mistaking it.

Aaron picked up speed, moving from the bedroom and out into the hall.

The sound of a door clicking open almost silently had him on guard but David appeared in the hall, his hair standing on end and Aaron knew he had come straight from bed.

David caught his eye, the look on his face told Aaron that he had heard the noise too. Admiration for his brother rose in Aaron's chest. David didn't have the training he did, for all intents and purposes David was a civilian and yet he was creeping down the hall.

They met at the top of the stairs and Aaron took the lead, his body moving soundlessly as he took the steps two at a time. He reached the entry hall and moved straight for the door, David moved behind him and Aaron trusted his brother enough to know that no matter what happened, David would defend the girls.

Keeping his body low, Aaron peered out through the bottom of the window near the front door. As far as he could tell there was no one on the porch but as he dropped his gaze he spotted the package sitting on the doorstep and his heart dropped.

Movement across the other end of the porch had Aaron springing into action. Dragging the door open soundlessly he was out and across the porch before David even had the opportunity to react.

The figure was dressed head to toe in black and the moment he saw Aaron coming he started to run.

Leveraging his body against the railing on the wrap around porch Aaron boosted himself over the top, dropping down into the grass easily before he started to run.

The other man wasn't disciplined and Aaron didn't have to even push himself to catch up to him. He tackled him to the ground, their bodies colliding as he pushed the other man beneath him.

The masked figure grunted as he thrust his elbow upwards sharply in an attempt to catch Aaron in the face but it was pointless. Aaron moved swiftly, wrapping his hands around the other man's arms as he pressed them high up his back.

The man on the ground whimpered his body going rigid as Aaron pushed hard enough on the other man's joints to feel them teeter on the verge of snapping.

"What are you doing here?"

Aaron demanded, his voice hoarse with emotion.

"I was just dropping something off, man, I swear that was it! Please!"

His voice sounded young to Aaron's ears, immature and he released his arms suddenly and ripped the mask from his head. The boy couldn't have been more than eighteen or nineteen and Aaron felt his heart sink in his chest.

If Hank was using teens as his messengers then it meant the kid on the ground wouldn't know anything.

Aaron rolled up onto his feet and reached down, grabbing the boy by the back of his neck as he tugged him to his feet.

There were tears in the teens eyes and Aaron could see the tracks of them down his face as he fought to keep his balance.

"Why were you dropping something off in the middle of the night?"

Aaron shook the boy a little more gently as he turned him back towards the house.

There were other lights on now and two of the security guards were making their way across the lawn towards Aaron and the boy.

Anger rose in Aaron chest and he had the sudden urge to fire the guards on the spot. He hired them to protect his family and they'd let him down.

"Sir?"

The bolder of the guards stepped forward as though he planned on taking the boy into his custody. Aaron shook his head sharply, his eyes narrowed.

"Get the hell out of my house and take all of your crap with you."

The guards stared at him, their faces stunned as they struggled to take in his words."

"Mr Ashcroft, I…"

"Where the hell were you? Where were you while he was creeping around on the porch leaving boxes from Hank?"

"Something knocked out the security cameras at the back of the house and we went to check on it…"

Aaron shook his head.

"Not good enough. You have one job and that's to guard the house and the occupants. You screwed up and I want you gone and don't think you'll be getting any references from me either…"

The silent guard didn't say anything, biting his tongue as he turned and headed back in the direction of the house once more. The other guard who had spoken to begin with opened his mouth to pipe up once more.

Aaron glared at him, his stare withering and yet the other man held his ground. The boy in Aaron's grip struggled suddenly forcing Aaron's attention back to him as he whined.

"You're hurting me, you don't need to hurt me, I won't do nothin'."

Aaron started forward when the guard grabbed his arm forcing him to come to a halt.

"You're making a huge mistake, I think you need a minute to reconsider."

Aaron sucked in a deep breath drawing the air in through his nose before releasing it. He levelled his gaze on the other man, giving him the full weight of his hard eyes.

"I don't need any time to think about it. I can't trust you to protect the people I love, if I can't trust you to do that, then you're pointless and I want you gone. Now if I were you, I'd get your hand off my arm and I'd follow your buddy back to the house to get your stuff."

The guard's face shifted suddenly, his already angry eyes snapping with rage as he lashed out. But his body gave him away and Aaron saw the blow coming. He released the boy long enough to dodge the punch.

Aaron's hand came back up automatically, his punch sharp and forceful as it landed squarely on the other man's face. There was a distinct crunch and Aaron couldn't help but feel a small modicum of satisfaction as he watched the other man crumple to the ground.

Blood gushed from his nose as he pressed his hands to his face, or at least Aaron assumed it was blood but it was too dark to be fully sure. The boy stood and watched, his mouth hanging open. The moment he saw Aaron turning back to him he lifted his hands as though in surrender.

"I swear I won't run, you don't need to do that to me!"

If it had been over anything else Aaron might have found the panicked look the boy was giving him funny. But this was related to Hank and Aaron couldn't see the humour in any part of it. Hank was attempting to rip his life apart and whether the boy liked it or not he was now apart of it.

"Move, to the house, now."

Aaron kept his commands short and concise as he raised his arm and pointed in the direction of the house. The teen didn't need to be told twice and he scuttled in the direction of the house as fast as his legs would carry him.

Aaron strode after him, leaving the guard on the ground to moan into his hands.

Aaron reached the edge of the porch, the boy stood waiting on the steps for him, his hands twisting nervously in the black jumper he wore. David stood out on the porch, his arms folded across his chest and the expression he wore was anything but friendly.

"You fired the guards?"

They were the first words out of David's mouth as Aaron stepped onto the porch. It made him pause and he stared up at the defiant look on his brother's face. Aaron simply nodded, he didn't need to explain himself to David, not in his own house.

David stared at him for a moment before he nodded, his expression lightening.

"Good, because I wasn't sure how you'd take to me firing your guards in your own home."

"If they deserved to be fired then I wouldn't have a problem."

"And the beating?"

David jerked his head in the direction of the man still hunched over in the lawn.

Aaron shrugged as he moved up the steps pushing the boy ahead of him.

"He started it and I finished it, what was I supposed to do?"

David laughed and Aaron fought to keep his own smile under wraps. The last thing he needed was to find pleasure in beating down on someone else.

The sight of the package quickly killed all joy Aaron might have felt. It sank down inside him, crushed beneath the weight of whatever he would find in the parcel. The last two had been bad enough and each one seemed to only get worse. Whatever this one contained, Aaron knew it would be brutal and he dreaded the moment when he would have to open it.

He swallowed hard in an attempt to push his emotions down inside. He would need to be as cold as possible if he was going to look at whatever perverse gift Hank had sent him.

"Aaron, what's going on?"

The sound of Heather's voice from the top of the stairs froze the blood in Aaron's veins. She couldn't see the package. Whatever else she learned, the contents of Hank's gift was not on the list.

Chapter Two

*S*TANDING AT THE TOP OF the stairs I could still see Aaron's expression the moment I called out to him. There was clearly something wrong but that was apparent in the fact that he was escorting a young kid into his study. David stepped in through the front door and my heart slowed in my chest.

If David was with him then whatever was going on couldn't be too terrible... Or at least I hoped it couldn't be.

"David, what are you doing outside? Who's the boy?"

I started down the stairs, drawing my dressing gown in around my body a little tighter. The cool night air was still flooding in through the gaping front door and the moment I reached the ground floor I started towards it, my hand reaching out to shut it.

"Heather, you should go back to bed, it's nothing, really."

The tone in Aaron's voice let me know immediately that he was lying. The realisation that he was keeping things from me cut me to the core and I struggled to keep my expression calm.

"I'm not going back to bed when clearly there's something going on? Who's the boy?"

Aaron stared at me, his mouth opening and closing as he struggled to find an answer he could give me.

"We heard him prowling around outside…"

David cut in, spreading his hands wide as he stepped in front of Aaron and the boy.

"And what? You both went to investigate instead of the security team doing it?"

David was harder to read but I had a feeling that he was covering for Aaron. There was something they didn't want me to know and I couldn't put my finger on it but whatever it was, it was clearly serious.

"Something like that."

David grinned at me but I wasn't falling for it. I sidestepped him, and paused as I came face to face with Aaron. He wore a guilty expression and for the life of me I couldn't figure out why he'd be looking at me like that.

My gaze darted from Aaron and came to rest on the box that sat on the hall table just inside the door. The moment I saw it I felt my stomach lurch as I remembered the last one.

Aaron had tried to keep all of Hank's correspondence from me but there was only so much he could hide. I'd seen the lock of Kirsty's hair, the blood smeared note and it was enough to know that Hank was truly psycho sick.

Of course Aaron had kept all of the video confessions from me but he couldn't stop me from listening at the doors when he called the police around and put the tape on for them. The screaming wasn't something I could get out of my head and I was certain I never would.

"He wasn't just a prowler was he? Hank sent him?"

I couldn't tear my gaze away from the parcel on the table, my eyes raking over its perfectly wrapped exterior. How he managed to seal up each box without ever leaving trace evidence was beyond me. How could he be so good at hiding from the police, from Aaron and all while he taunted them.

"Yeah, I heard him leaving the parcel. I'm going to call the cops and get them out here but not before I ask him some questions of my own."

"What sort of questions?"

My voice sounded a little hollow as I turned my gaze back to Aaron. The boy stood in the doorway to the study, the expression he wore one of complete terror. The moment I focused in on the boy I felt all of my emotions flooding back to me. They crowded into my head almost as though they could crowd out all of my logical thoughts.

"He's just a kid, what's he going to know?"

"I don't know, Heather but the least little thing could be important and we need to know everything."

"I want to sit in on it, I want to know what he has to say."

Aaron instantly shook his head and moved to stand between me and the door.

"No, Heather, you know you can't. We don't know what he's going to say and I don't…"

I cut him off my voice going hard.

"You don't want what? You don't want me to know how dangerous Hank is? How completely insane he is? I think it's a little late for all of that. I already know he's mad, I already know that the things he's doing to Kirsty would very probably scar me for life and yet I have to know…"

"Heather, I really can't let you… I don't want you knowing this, I don't want you knowing what I know, carrying what I have to carry. I don't want to have to watch it rip you apart too."

"So what? I'm supposed to sit idly by, twiddling my thumbs as I watch the guilt eat you alive? Aaron Ashcroft, I love you but I won't be wrapped in cotton wool while you suffer through all the difficult times."

"Heather, he's not alone, he has me. I'm here no matter what and I'll always stick by him, especially for something like this. I'll make sure he doesn't get in to deep."

I shook my head as I turned towards David, I knew he meant well and that every word he spoke was sincere but none of it mattered. He couldn't protect Aaron from it, not in the way he needed to be protected. I wasn't even sure I could but I sure as hell knew that I could stand by his side and be there every step of the way. And when the nightmares stole him from my bed at night then I would be there to hold him and listen when he was good and ready to talk about it. But I couldn't do any of that if he spent his time trying to protect me.

"David, I know you love your brother but you and I both know that you can't be there during the darkest hours but I can... You just need to trust me."

"Heather, I do trust you."

Aaron's voice was choked as he stepped forward and wrapped me in his arms. I let him hold me, his grip tightening to almost painful proportions as he clung to me.

"Then don't shut me out. Let me sit in on your questioning."

Aaron didn't answer me, instead he pulled back and stared down into my face. He seemed to study me for a moment before finally nodding his head.

"Fine, but you can't interfere."

I nodded suddenly unsure of the man standing in front of me. Why did he need my assurance that I wouldn't interfere? Why was that so important? What did he have planned?

I glanced over Aaron's shoulder and stared at the teen who stood awkwardly in the door to the study. The look he gave me made me want to reach out to him and tell him that everything would be alright. I wanted to reassure him, tell him that if he just answered all of Aaron's questions that everything would be fine and yet I knew I couldn't do that.

He might have been a child but he had agreed to work with Hank. He had gotten the package from somewhere and he agreed to come to our house in the middle of the night. If Hank had asked him to do anything else part of me couldn't help but wonder if he would have carried out his orders?

Chapter Three

STARING OVER HEATHER'S SHOULDER AARON caught sight of David shaking his head as though attempting to discourage him from allowing Heather to sit in. But what the hell was he supposed to do? It would have been different if she had stayed upstairs for the entire time but she hadn't and there was nothing he could do about that now.

Squaring his shoulders Aaron turned back to the kid standing in the door. In the full light of the hall he seemed younger somehow and Aaron had a moment of doubt. Maybe it would be better to simply call the cops and let them deal with him. But then Aaron knew if he did that he would always regret losing the opportunity to question him. It was important to get the answers to the questions that were plaguing him.

He needed to know where he'd come into contact with Hank, it was possible it could mean something to Aaron but the police could dismiss it as unimportant. The only way this case would be cracked is if he had every single piece of information he could get his hands on. And sometimes that meant doing things that went against his better judgement.

"In and sit."

Aaron barked his orders at the teen who stood in the doorway with a terrified expression on his face. He went without argument dropping into the first seat he came across. Aaron fought not to turn and look at Heather for moral support. He desperately wanted to, he wanted to see the look on her face. He wanted to know exactly what she thought of him. But Aaron knew that if there was any uncertainty in her eyes that he wouldn't be able to do what needed to be done. And he couldn't risk her or Arianna because he was afraid of what Heather thought of him.

Realisation hit Aaron as he walked into the room and took his place against the edge of the desk, he would rather be hated by her than lose her because of a failure to protect her when he had the opportunity. It was a difficult and painful realisation but one he desperately needed to have.

"What's your name?"

Aaron kept his voice low but there was a threat in his tone.

The teen stared up at him with wide and frightened blue eyes but something lurked just beneath the surface that Aaron couldn't quite get a lock on.

"You have to call the cops, you can't keep me here…"

Aaron smiled but it wasn't a pleasant look and it made the youngster shift uncomfortably in his chair.

"Until I call the cops you're my guest and I can ask whatever questions I want to ask."

"And I don't have to tell you jack shit."

Aaron's gaze shifted to David who was leaning against the closed door with his arms folded casually across his chest. He wore a lazy smile but Aaron knew that was simply covering the irritation he felt, an irritation they shared.

"Where did you get the package?"

"What package?"

The kid leaned back in the seat, his body relaxing as though he had them all figured out. Hank had obviously told him something, probably that he would be perfectly safe, the cops would be called and he'd be released as long as he pretended complete innocence.

Aaron moved across the room, the anger he felt bubbling to the surface and making him move far faster than the teen was prepared for.

Aaron wrapped his fist into the boy's black hooded jumper and jerked him forward forcing extreme close quarters eye contact.

"I know he told you that with me you'd be safe. That I wouldn't touch you, that I was one of the good guys but

Hank forgot one very crucial detail in all of this." Aaron jerked his head in the direction of where Heather stood and the kid rolled his eyes up to stare at her.

"He forgot about her, he forgot that I have people I love, people I would die for, people I would kill for. Hank has spent too long apart from me and he forgets how fiercely loyal I am once I find something worth protecting."

"He said you couldn't touch me, that you were in the public eye too much and you couldn't risk laying hands on me or it'd mess up your businesses... That it would turn the cops against you."

Aaron grinned but it was more a barring of his teeth.

"I don't need to do anything to you tonight. The moment you walk out of here with the cops I can wash my hands of you but if you haven't told me anything useful..."

Aaron trailed off and let the silence speak for his intentions instead.

The kid swallowed hard, his eyes darting back and forth as though he was searching for some way out. Aaron had him and he knew it, he could practically feel the moment when he decided to share what he knew.

Aaron released him as suddenly as he'd grabbed him, letting him drop back into the chair but Aaron didn't move from his position in front of him. He stared down at him as he folded his arms.

"So what's your name?"

"Karl, Karl Johnson."

Aaron shook his head. "Is that you're real name? It sounds a lot like a pretend name."

"It's my name now. I've lived on the street for nearly nine years and that was the name I picked for myself... It's anonymous enough for me incase I get picked up by the cops."

Aaron sighed and slowly retreated back to the desk. Pressing him for his real name was nothing but a waste of time. It was something the cops could do if they really wanted to.

"Where did you get the package?"

"He gave it to me."

"Hank? You saw Hank?"

Karl shook his head. "Dunno, never gave me his name."

Aaron could feel his irritation rising again. The more he tried to figure out what Karl was holding back from him the harder it was to focus in on. Aaron knew he was lying but how was he supposed to know what he was lying about when everything that came out of his mouth felt like a half truth.

"Why does it feel like you're covering for him, Karl?"

David pushed away from the door and sauntered into the centre of the room. He was the epitome of calm and yet Aaron knew that he was feeling anything but calm. The only thing that gave David away was the look in his eyes. David was the one person who understood what the fear was like, the need to protect those you loved.

"I'm not, I swear, he never gave me his name. I don't know who he is…"

"Then where did you meet him? How does he contact you? Do you know where he's hiding out?" Aaron pushed away from the desk and stood a little taller.

"Hiding? He's not hiding, or at least not that I can tell. He approached me on the street, said he had a job for me. I thought he was just some dude who was looking for the types of things I'm not into but he said he knew who I was… He could tell me all sorts of crazy things about my past. So when he told me about the job, that it was just dropping the package off outside the house and he paid me half now, with the other half to come after, I decided what the hell."

Aaron walked around the desk and turned the key in his top drawer of his desk. He tugged a brown folder from beneath a stack of papers and closed the drawer. Walking back around the desk he dropped the folder onto Karl's lap and stood watching him closely.

"What's this?"

"Open it."

Aaron kept his voice even and low, never taking his eyes from the boy's face. He wanted to see his reaction, to take in every little nuance of his behaviour. Karl flipped the folder open and the tossed the file onto the floor as soon as his eyes focused in on the picture. He hopped up from his chair, lifting his hands as though to ward off whatever Aaron was going to say to him next.

"Look, man, I don't know what you're in to but you can't do that to me... You can't threaten me with shit like that..."

Reaching down Aaron scooped the folder up from the floor and pulled another picture out from deeper in the pile of documents within.

"Karl, I'm not the threat. But I needed you to see that, I need to know the truth and I don't have time for your games. I need you to tell me if the man you got the package from was this man here."

Aaron held the picture of Hank out in front of him and waited for Karl to take it. It was then that Aaron made the mistake of glancing over in Heather's direction. Her face was a mix of shock and horror and Aaron could only hope that she hadn't caught sight of what the file contained. How could he explain the pictures he had gotten his hands on?

Aaron forced his gaze away from Heather and returned his attention back to Karl. The youngster hesitated, the look in his eyes one of genuine fear and Aaron knew for certain that he hadn't been expecting the graphic nature of the pictures.

Reaching out he snatched the picture Aaron held out to him, his gaze raking over the picture in front of him.

"Did he do that?"

Karl lifted his gaze from the picture long enough to ask the question.

"Yeah, but I need to know if that's the man that gave you the package?"

Karl nodded and Aaron felt his chest tighten. It was frustrating to be so close to Hank and yet so far from actually catching him.

"How did he plan to get the second half of your payment to you?"

"He said it would be waiting for me once I got back from dropping off your package."

"And if you were arrested?"

Aaron didn't believe for a moment that Hank actually planned on paying Karl the second half of his money. Hank had no reason to keep his word but it was still an avenue worth looking into.

"Then he'd keep it safe until I could get it."

Aaron smiled, "How about we let you go and you go and collect your money?"

The room immediately erupted with Heather and David arguing against the plan. Karl stood watching him carefully as though he was suddenly unsure about Aaron stability. And maybe he was right, maybe he was right to look at him as though he had just lost his marbles. There was no denying the fact that Karl needed to be handed over to the cops and if they knew that Aaron was considering risking him escaping they would be furious.

"Aaron, you can't be serious? It would be the worst possible thing that you could do, what if he gets away? All you'd have accomplished would be for nothing, Hank would know that you're not playing the game the way he thinks you are."

"He probably knows anyway, David, he's always been two steps ahead of us. The very last thing Hank will expect is that we would release the kid…"

The sound of knocking on the study door finished the conversation. David was the one standing closest to the door and he pulled it open. Aaron couldn't see the expression on his brother's face but he could tell from the way he stiffened his shoulders that something wasn't right.

David stood back from the door and Detective Bennet strode into the room. The look on his face instantly told Aaron that he knew what was going on.

"Aaron, I'm simply here as a courtesy because of what happened with Fossen. I told them down at the precinct that you contacted me about the package and your other guest. But they won't hang around for very long, you're supposed to call stuff like this in…"

Aaron lifted his hands and sat back on the edge of the desk.

"Claude, you know I would if I thought the police could get more information out of Karl here. I need to know where Hank is, I have to stop him, get to him before something really horrible happens…"

Aaron paused and then tilted his head to the side.

"Claude, how did you hear about this?"

The detective shifted uncomfortably his gaze dropping to the floor as he suddenly became fascinated by the pattern on the carpet.

"Claude, how the hell did you know?"

"He rang… He called the station up and asked us why we hadn't held a press conference about the package. He's getting braver, Aaron, and we need to play this one by the book. What was in the package?"

Aaron shrugged and shook his head.

"I don't know…"

Aaron's stomach churned uncomfortably as he realised that once again Hank had been one step ahead of them."

The sound of a muffled cry from the hall drew everyone's attention. David's face blanched suddenly and he was the first one out the door. Aaron was right behind him, his strides long and purposeful taking him straight out into the hallway.

Chapter Four

I FOLLOWED AARON AND DAVID out into the hall, knowing instinctively that the cry had come from Carrie. She was the only one not clued in on what was going on downstairs.

I stepped out into the hall in time to see David wrap his arms around Carrie's shoulders. Her face was pale and I could see a look of fear and disgust in her eyes. It took me a second to realise that she was looking past me to the place where the package was sitting.

I turned, my eyes trying to make sense of what I was looking at. Aaron's hands across my shoulders halted my movement and he tried to turn me away but I was determined. I wasn't the weakling that he and everyone else seemed to think I was, I was more than capable of dealing with what was going on.

"Aaron, what is it?"

The box that sat on the table was slowly beginning to change colour. Whatever was inside it was seeping through and I could see the small dark puddle that formed around it on the table top. My stomach churned. No one had even opened it yet and already I could feel myself wanting to get sick.

"Don't look at it, just ignore and go back into the study."

"What the hell was in that thing?"

Karl's voice cut across Aaron, forcing the rest of us to turn around and look at him. Was he telling the truth? Did he really have no idea what Hank was up to? Could he possibly have delivered the package and not have known what was inside it? It seemed so impossible and yet when Aaron had spoken to him he had maintained his innocence. What other choice was there but to believe him?

Detective Bennet approached it cautiously as though afraid it might blow up in his face. It seemed unlikely that Hank would do that, he enjoyed his games far too much to end them so abruptly.

"Has anyone else touched it?"

Detective Bennet crouched down and studied the package from all sides before once more straightening up.

"I had it brought in but the person who handled it wore gloves, you won't find any trace evidence from them."

Bennet nodded and pulled a pair of gloves from inside the jacket he wore. He dragged them on before reaching down and carefully tugging the lid open.

I fought my urge to take a step closer so I could see what lay inside the package but it was almost overwhelming in its intensity. I wanted to know what Hank was doing to Kirsty, it was a way of feeling responsible for her. I liked her and she didn't deserve what was happening to her.

Bennet took one stumbling step backwards and I hopped out of his way. Aaron's arms tightened on me, the tension in his body practically sang through his muscles and I knew he could see whatever was inside the box.

"Aaron, what is it?"

I whispered the words and I wasn't sure why but for some reason the moment felt as though it deserved whispering. As though whatever was inside the box was so terrible it couldn't be named aloud.

"I'm not rightly sure."

He was lying, lying to protect me but it was still a lie.

"Please, don't lie to me… You know what it is and unless you want me to go over there and look at it just tell me."

Aaron dropped his head down onto mine, his lips pressing to the top of my head as he kissed me softly.

"Sometimes you make it impossible to protect you."

"Sometimes you try and protect me when I don't need it."

"Can't you just trust me this time, Heather?"

He sounded suddenly tired and hearing it in his voice made me truly afraid. To hear the resignation from Aaron through his voice was terrifying. If even he was at a loss then how was anybody supposed to help Kirsty?

"Won't you trust me?"

He sighed again and I felt his shoulders drop.

"I won't tell you but I won't stop you from looking either. It's your choice at the end of the day and I won't stop you from doing the things you want to do, no matter how foolish I might think they are."

"Aaron, you can't be serious, you can't let her look at that."

There was horror in Detective Bennet's voice and for a cop who had seen truly terrible things I was surprised to know that a box could bother him so much.

Squaring my shoulders I stepped away from Aaron, one small hesitant step forward, then another and another. It was the stench that hit me first. It was like walking into a butcher shop, the smell of something raw and bloody.

The dark stain along the side of the box suddenly made sense. It was bleeding, not the box but whatever was inside it was bleeding. I struggled to keep my stomach in check as I took one final trembling step forward and peered into the box.

There was a small plastic lunch box lying at the bottom of the cardboard box. The lid was lifted away and I knew that the movement from its travels had obviously pushed the lid off. Part of me wondered if that wasn't

Hank's plan all along. It was possible that he had left the lid unsecured, forcing it to come loose.

I didn't need to push the lid from the top of the box to know what was inside it. I could see enough through the sides and top of the box to make an educated guess. I could remember taking biology, the teacher supplying us all with pig hearts to dissect and the feeling of nausea that had washed over me.

I turned and tears welled in my eyes as Aaron strode over to me and wrapped me in his arms.

"It's a heart, Aaron, he sent us a heart…"

My words came out in a garbled mess and I fought back the nausea that tried to overwhelm me. How could he do something like that? I didn't want to think of the heart belonging to anyone. What if it was Kirsty's heart? What if she was dead and now he planned on sending little bits of her to us in the mail?

It was something that didn't bear thinking about and yet I couldn't get it out of my head.

"I'm sorry, Heather, I'm so sorry…"

Aaron's voice was filled with emotion as he held me, rocking me against his body and I let him do it. In my mind I couldn't figure out why he was the one apologising, what did he have to be sorry about? I had the sudden need to hold Arianna in my arms, to feel her tiny warm body against my chest. I wanted to hear each little breath that she took, the tiny movements of her little hands.

"I just need to go and hold Arianna."

Aaron nodded as he continued to hold me and when he drew away I saw a look in his eyes that I'd never noticed before. There was a guilt there that I couldn't fathom. What reason did he have to feel guilty about what was going on? None of it made any sense.

I lifted my hand and pressed my palm against his cheek. I watched him close his eyes and lean into my touch. I wanted to ask him about the look in his eyes but there was too many people around and now didn't seem like the right time.

"Go and hold, Arianna, I'll be up as soon as I can."

He released me and I headed for the stairs. Turning I caught Aaron's gaze on me, his eyes were filled with an intensity that frightened me and I suddenly realised that he intended on going to any lengths to protect us from Hank.

Carrie joined me on the stairs and I caught sight of the paleness of her face as we climbed the steps.

"Are you alright?"

It was such an inadequate question and yet it was the only one I could think to ask.

She shot me a look with her wide frightened eyes and nodded quickly.

"Yeah, I'm fine, it was just a surprise is all. I didn't expect to come down and see that…"

She trailed off and returned her gaze to the steps.

"Was it really a heart?"

Her question surprised me and the moment she asked it I felt myself stumble. I caught myself before I fell forward onto the steps and Carrie automatically reached out to me, her hand holding me in place.

"I'm ok now, thanks."

I nodded but it was more a reassurance for myself than for her. The moment she had said 'heart' an image of it popped into my head. It was something that would stay with me for a long time to come and I had no idea how I was supposed to shake something like that. I could practically imagine what the nightmares would look like and I dreaded the thought of even closing my eyes.

"Yeah, it was... It might not be human..."

I wasn't sure why I added the extra sentence and as we reached the top of the steps Carrie groaned. She leaned against the banister her already pale face taking on an unhealthy glow.

"Carrie, what's wrong?"

She shook her head and clutched the edge of the banister with her eyes shut.

"I'm fine, it's just a little bit of morning sickness made worse by what's downstairs..."

She trailed off again and I could see the tiny beads of sweat the broke out on her forehead. I knew that look, I'd suffered through it myself carrying Arianna and I wouldn't have wished it on my worst enemy.

Linking my arm through hers I propelled her down the hall towards the main bathroom. She clutched at the

35

door gratefully and disappeared inside. I let her go, knowing that in that moment privacy was best.

Returning to Arianna's room I pushed the door open gently and stepped inside. The room was lit by the soft glow of her little night light and as I crept into the room she stirred in her sleep.

I perched over her crib, staring down at her tiny perfect body, her little hands balled into fists as she slept. Reaching down I scooped her up and pressed her to my chest. She was warm and when I dipped my nose down to the small little bit of fuzzy hair on the top of her head I couldn't help but smile.

She smelled warm and as I carried her over to the rocking chair in the corner I drank in her scent. Holding Arianna in my arms was the only true way I knew of chasing away all the bad memories that tried to crowd my mind. With her in my arms the world had a way of suddenly righting itself, I felt safer. I was her mother and I comforted her but on some of the dark nights I'd gone through I'd discovered that she was my comfort too.

The door creaked open and Aaron slipped inside. He looked exhausted and I instantly wished the chair was big enough for him to sit too. He moved across the room and stood over me, the shadow he cast obstructing a clear view of his face.

Without a word he dropped to the floor, pressing his back against my legs as he reached up with his arm and placed his hand on Arianna's foot. We sat there in the half dark, the only sound was the contended little snores of our daughter. Her innocence helped us to find a way to deal with what was going on. Or at least that was how I imagined it.

"Bennet is taking the package and Karl back to the station. He's called for forensics to come out and gather what they can before it gets moved."

"What'll happen to Karl?"

Aaron sighed and dropped his head back against my knees. He stared up at the ceiling for a few moments before finally answering me.

"The cops will hold him for a while, he'll plead guilty to trespassing but that's about it. He didn't actually do anything wrong…"

"He worked with Hank, is that not bad?"

I couldn't keep the sarcasm from my voice and Arianna stirred in my grip once more as though disturbed by my tone.

"Heather, you know what I think about this situation. If I could get more out of him… If we could have just taken him back to the money we might have picked up something. Hank is going to make a mistake somewhere, somehow, I just don't know when and I'd rather it was sooner instead of later."

We both fell silent. I listened to the soft breathing of our child but my mind kept on straying back to what I'd seen downstairs. I didn't regret looking, Hank was capable of terrible things and I couldn't afford to be squeamish about them.

"Do you think it was her heart?"

Aaron didn't answer me immediately and I could practically hear the thoughts churning in his mind. We could both hope and pray that it wasn't a piece of Kirsty in the box but if it wasn't then it meant it was a piece of someone else. Hank had Kirsty but if he'd grown bored of her and she was dead then where was her body?

"I really don't know."

The sound of cars drawing into the driveway drew our attention to the window. Aaron stood and made his way across the room, he pulled back the curtains and stared out through the clear glass. His shoulders were tense, his body rigid.

"Aaron, what was that look about earlier?"

"What look?"

He turned back to me but I couldn't read the expression on his face in the darkness.

"When you looked at me downstairs after you said you were sorry…"

I trailed off but Aaron was silent. I could feel the heavy gaze of his eyes on my face as he watched me. I wasn't sure if I was supposed to continue trying to explain to him about the look but part of me knew that he understood.

He sighed and started towards the door.

"I better go and see if they need my help…"

"Aaron, aren't you even going to answer me?"

"About what, Heather, I don't know what look you're talking about."

His voice was sharp and I knew that my question had thrown him completely off guard but I hadn't expected such an extreme reaction. I recoiled away from him, my grip tightening on Arianna. She stirred again in my arms, gurgling as she started to wake up.

I stared down at her and before I had the chance to react Aaron pulled the bedroom door open and slipped out into the hall. He closed the door silently behind him and I watched it until it clicked shut. I wanted to go after him, demand an answer. I'd waited until we were away from everyone else, I hadn't questioned him in front of his brother or the detective. The way he had reacted to me wasn't right and I struggled to wrap my head around his reasoning. There had been no mistaking the look in his eyes and his reaction had confirmed it. What was I supposed to think?

A knock so quiet I almost missed it had me moving for the door. I pulled it open and Carrie stood on the other side. Her face was still pale but she didn't look as ill as she had earlier. Smiling I stepped aside and she followed me into the room.

"David, told me to stay up here. I don't particularly want to but I don't think my stomach could handle what's downstairs…"

I nodded sympathetically and gestured for her to take a seat in the rocking chair. She dropped down into it and reached her hands out. I passed Arianna to her, watching as she lifted her carefully into her arms and held her against her body. Arianna fussed, her tiny hands beating against Carrie as she struggled to find just the right place to once more fall back to sleep. She was the epitome of a perfect angel and I could imagine what she would be like once she got a little older. The phrase, 'butter wouldn't melt' sprang to mind.

"She's always so quiet."

Carrie's voice was filled with reverence as she cradled Arianna against her body.

"Not always, when she's hungry she screams like a banshee."

My lips curled in a smile and without really thinking about what I was doing I moved to the window. I stood in the same spot Aaron had and pulled the curtains aside. I stared down into the circular drive, the lazy blue and red flash of cop cars lighting everything up.

I'd imagined my life with Aaron but if I was honest with myself this scene had never played a part in my dreams. What had we done to deserve the constant upheaval? Would there ever be a time when our lives would be our own?

I was desperate to get away from it all and just enjoy the life I was building with Aaron and our child. I watched as Aaron moved down the steps outside and my heart ached in my chest. I wanted him to share his thoughts with me, to let me understand what was going on inside his mind. I knew it was the only way I was going to find any peace of mind. And deep down I knew until he opened up to me completely he wouldn't find any peace either.

Chapter Five

ETECTIVE BENNET STOOD OUTSIDE WITH the police officers that had arrived. Aaron watched him closely, studying his body language as he gave instructions to the officers in uniform.

Aaron wanted to trust him, he wanted to believe that Bennet was one of the good guys, that he would do whatever it took to bring Hank down. Yet there was something inside Aaron that niggled at him, a feeling that Bennet didn't have it in him to go the extra mile. Of course there was no way to prove it and part of Aaron wondered if maybe he was simply being unfair to the other man. It certainly wouldn't have been the first time that he held someone to an impossible standard and found them lacking.

"That's not a good look."

David's voice cut through Aaron's intense thoughts and drew him back into the moment.

"What look would that be?"

Aaron turned as his brother propped himself against the doorframe a large glass of scotch in his hand.

"I see you found my stash."

Aaron gestured to the glass in his brother's hand, his tone dry.

"It wasn't exactly hard, you're a little predictable, Aaron, you hide everything precious in the same place."

Aaron couldn't help but feel himself bristle with irritation. He was glad to have David around, to have him planted firmly on his side, David wasn't the type of man he would wish as an enemy. But it didn't change the fact that sometimes he was down right irritating.

"What the hell does that mean?"

David smiled and stood, he emptied the glass with one long swallow before he answered.

"Hank wants to hurt you. I don't know why but you've obviously pissed him off in some way so he wants to get at you. The best way to do that is to get at the things you hold dear. He knew by sending the package to your home that it would put you on the defensive, make you tense and cause you to act rashly."

"If you mean my plan to take Karl back to the money…"

David nodded.

"Yeah, think logically for a moment, Aaron. If you had gone with Karl where would the people you value most in your life be? Where would Heather and Arianna be?"

Aaron swallowed hard and scrubbed his hands over his eyes. David wasn't making any sense and yet Aaron knew deep down that the words leaving David's mouth were making perfect sense, he just needed to stop and think about them. Really think about it.

"They would have been here with a house full of guards..."

"You already fired two guards tonight based on their lack of attention. Do you really think the guards could stand against Hank?"

"You think he was here all along?"

Aaron could feel the colour drain from his face. It wasn't something he had even thought about. The entire thing was a set up. It stank to high heavens and he hadn't even seen it.

"Hank knows you, Aaron, almost as well as I do. Sometimes I think he knows you better, you have so much in common."

"I'm nothing like that bastard."

"No, you're not a murderer but you both shared something, something you refuse to let anyone else in on. When you worked together there were things you both witnessed that only another person in that position would understand... You've never let anyone else in on that, Aaron, not even Heather."

"You don't understand, I couldn't tell her about that… If I did she'd hate me, you all would…"

Aaron let his voice trail off. Memories surface in his head, memories he struggled to push back behind the wall he had built inside his own mind. A wall he needed if he was going to function. There were some things in this world that no one should have to witness and Aaron knew if he allowed the memories to bleed into the rest of his head he wouldn't ever come back.

A hand dropped onto Aaron's shoulder and he tensed, his entire body going rigid. It took him a moment to realise the hand belonged to David. He sucked in a deep breath, forcing it into his lungs, forcing his body to release the tension that threatened to eat him alive. It had taken him a long time to stop his body from instinctually reacting. And the moment Hank had gone off the reservation Aaron had found himself falling back into old habits.

If he'd allowed his body to react the way it had wanted to, he knew David would be currently cradling a broken arm. Aaron lifted his gaze to his brother's face and the look he saw there surprised him. David knew the risk he had taken, he knew what Aaron was capable of and yet he had still reached out to him…

"I think you could tell Heather anything… She loves you, nothing can change that. After everything you two have been through to doubt her is stupid."

"I could say the same to you."

Aaron quipped back, forcing his surprise and anger, his instincts to react back behind the wall in his head. He let out a long breath as his body slowly returned to normal and he let the tension in his shoulders flood away.

David grinned at him before dropping his gaze sheepishly to the floor.

"I know... I'm speaking to you from experience. I've learned my lesson the hard way and well if I can save you the hassle."

Aaron smiled and turned back to the door.

"So what did you mean when you said it wasn't a 'good look'?"

David moved up beside him and they stared out into the darkness. The night was cast in an odd glow with the constant flare of red and blue lights from the cars parked across the driveway.

"You were watching him as though he was the one who had left the package on the doorstep."

"I'm not sure if I can trust him, I'm not sure if I want to trust him."

"If you can't trust him then who will you trust? He's one of the good guys, Aaron, he's a cop, if you need anyone on your side right now it's him."

Aaron sighed and dropped his gaze to his fists, he slowly curled them until his knuckles changed colour from red to white. He released the tension suddenly, letting it flow out of him as he started down the steps and towards Bennet.

"Detective, can we have a little chat?"

Bennet turned towards him a look of surprise covering his face as he watched Aaron stride towards him.

"I didn't think there was anything to discuss, Aaron." Bennet dropped his voice and leaned in towards Aaron, his voice taking on an angry tone. "I know you didn't plan on calling me and I have no idea what game you think you're playing but I refuse to get caught up in it, Ashcroft."

Aaron smiled but it wasn't a friendly look, instead he plastered it on his face for the benefit of the officers who were watching them carefully from nearby.

"Do you really want to do this in front of your men, Bennet?"

"I don't want to do this anywhere. I just need you to promise me that you'll stay the hell out of this investigation from now on."

Aaron shook his head, his smile slipping a little.

"I can't do that and you know it. I know Hank better than anyone, you need me and you know it."

"I don't need you fucking everything up. There's a girl missing and I can only hope to God that what's in that box isn't hers because I'll be the one explaining to her parents if it is…"

Bennet trailed off and scrubbed his hand over his face as though through that action alone he could wipe the memory of the horror of what lay in the box from his head. But Aaron knew it was impossible. Once you had seen it, once your brain had figured out what it was looking at there was no going back. The image would forever be seared into Detective Bennet's head and Aaron suddenly found himself feeling sorry for the other man.

"Is that your first time for something like this?"

Aaron softened his voice, he didn't want Bennet to know that he pitied him but he wanted him to know that he could empathise with what he was going through. The first few horrors Aaron had witnessed had been the worst, after that he'd found a way to cope with it, throwing himself into the bottom of a bottle until Heather had come along and dragged him back out.

"I've seen bodies before but not like that… It's not even a body but I just can't wrap my head around what it takes to do something like that… What sort of a man can cut the heart out of another human being?"

Bennet's eyes were round and as the blue and red lights flashed around the drive they lit the white in his eye. There was a little too much white in his eye and Aaron knew he was in shock. It was strange to witness it in a cop. Bennet was old enough to have come across a lot of gruesome crimes and yet the box and its contents had clearly pushed him beyond his capabilities.

"Come inside and have something to steady your nerve, Bennet."

Aaron reached out to him and Bennet instantly shrugged out of his grip. There was another flash of the white of his eye and Aaron suddenly realised that reaching out to him had been a mistake. What the hell was making him act like this? What had spooked him so badly?

"Bennet, you need to get a grip on yourself. You can't let this get the better of you…"

"I don't need your pity, Ashcroft, if you had been honest with me in the first place, if you had come to me the moment you suspected your friend of something like this then we could have stopped it. Instead you had to play the big man and now the innocent are playing your price."

Bennet turned on his heel and strode away, leaving Aaron to watch after him. Aaron could see the tension in the other man's shoulders, he practically vibrated with the energy that rolled through him and Aaron felt a nervous knot start in his gut.

The last time he'd ignored his instincts Hank had gotten away. If he ignored his instincts this time then what would happen?

But what the hell was he supposed to do? Bennet was a cop and Aaron had no control over him. In fact, Bennet was the commanding officer at the scene, there was no one higher than him, no one Aaron could turn to with his suspicions. Even if there was, would they believe him? Probably not, cops didn't like to doubt their own and for good reason. When they were out on the street they had to trust that they had each other's backs. There could be no room for doubt or uncertainty.

"Shit."

Aaron muttered beneath his breath as he watched Bennet move towards a car parked at the far end of the drive. Karl sat in the back seat, his gaze lowered as he waited to be taken to the police station. Within a few hours he would be out once more, back on the street and free to work as Hank's errand boy until Hank grew tired of him.

Bennet slid in behind the wheel of the car and Aaron was forced to watch him go. The man was too highly strung and there was something that Aaron was missing, he just couldn't figure out what it was.

"Aaron."

David's voice rang out across the drive and Aaron took his eyes from Bennet and the car he was leaving in. Something niggled at Aaron and part of him wondered if he should follow the other man in. There was something he was missing and Aaron wasn't the type of man who enjoyed being in the dark, especially over something so important.

He reached the bottom of the steps in time to catch David's last words to one of the uniform cops.

"Where the hell are we supposed to go then?"

"What's wrong?"

Aaron moved up onto the first step as the officer turned and lifted his hands as though he could ward him off.

"I need you all to back off, this entire place has already been contaminated and what little evidence might have been here is practically destroyed."

"What evidence? The only real evidence is already headed back to the police station."

"That's only part of it, looks like whoever left the parcel on the doorstep left something else."

"Something else like what?"

Aaron's stomach churned and he knew whatever the cop was going to tell him wasn't something he would like.

"There's a listening device. We picked up the signal for this one but it's not the only one…"

"There are more?"

Aaron could feel the colour draining from his face. His house was compromised. It didn't seem possible and it shouldn't have been possible and yet if he was to believe the cop standing in front of him then it was true.

"Karl, couldn't have planted it, he didn't have enough time."

"But he was the one who left the package?" The cop furrowed his brow as he gestured for one of the other officers to come and help him.

David folded his arms across his chest and moved to the top of the steps. Aaron knew it was a way to simultaneously get out of their way and still remain close enough to get a good look at whatever they were doing. It was the exact thing he would have done if he had been standing where his brother was.

"He was the one who left the package but I heard him. He didn't have enough time to plant anything here or anywhere else."

Aaron watched as the cop opened his mouth as though to argue with him. It was utterly pointless to try and explain to them, they wouldn't understand, hell most of them didn't even believe Hank was as bad as Aaron had explained him to be.

Part of Aaron couldn't blame them for that belief. Hank was supposed to be one of the good guys. They were all supposed to work on the same side and follow the same rules and laws. They were all fighting for the same thing after all, or at least that was how the cops viewed the situation. They were missing one important piece of the puzzle, a piece none of them wanted to know about.

Just because you fought on the same side didn't make you good. The reason Aaron and Hank and others like them had been chosen was because they were good at killing. Cops weren't good at killing, it wasn't why they became cops and so they struggled to understand the motives of those who were different.

David moved down the steps drawing Aaron away to the side. The cop on the top of the wrap around porch watched them, Aaron could practically feel the weight of his curious gaze on the back of his neck. For a second Aaron wondered would he follow them in an attempt to continue the conversation, to argue his point.

"You agree with me now don't you?"

David, didn't have to explain his point, Aaron knew exactly what his brother was talking about.

"Yeah, I see it now. Hank was here, and if we're to believe the cops then he was also in the house."

"We don't know that for certain. If he planted enough listening devices around the outside it would allow him to hear what was going on inside."

Aaron shook his head.

"No, Hank isn't like that. The device the cops have found is to throw us off the trail. He knows me, he knows that I would sweep for crap like that and he knows my men would find them. This way he can make us believe that he never got inside the house, that everything he has done has been external..."

David shook his head, his expression growing more and more concerned as Aaron spoke.

"I don't like to think of him inside, Carrie, is in there, she's carrying my child and if he touches her..."

David trailed off as though suddenly realising the fruitlessness of his words. Aaron wanted to comfort his brother, tell him that everyone they cared about, everyone they loved would be safe. But he couldn't do that, it would all be lies and Aaron wasn't about to start lying to his brother.

"When do you think he put them there?"

Aaron shrugged and scrubbed his hands over his face. The constant lack of sleep ever since Hank had taken Kirsty was rapidly beginning to wear him down. And it terrified Aaron to think that Hank might do something and he would miss it, all because he was too tired to properly concentrate.

"I really don't know, I don't imagine he was brave enough to do it with us here?"

David nodded, but the look on his face told Aaron that he was clearly lost in thought.

"Do you think the cops will find them all?"

Aaron shook his head, a grim smile cross his face. It would be impossible for the cops to find everything and Aaron knew that from past experience. When Kirsty had gone missing they had refused to let him assist them in any way. He'd waited until they'd declared her house clear and then he'd gone in with his men, sweeping the place looking for something, anything that might give him a clue as to what Hank planned.

The listening devices placed in Kirsty's house had surprised him. What surprised Aaron more was the fact that Hank had felt cocky enough to leave them behind. It had shown just how secure he felt in his ability to outsmart everyone else.

"They didn't even find the ones he'd left in Kirsty's. The only reason they found this one is because Hank wanted them to."

"So what are we supposed to do? We need to tell the girls that they need to be guarded in what they say until we know the house is clear."

"I think you can do that…"

David stared intently at Aaron as though trying to ascertain what he was thinking simply by looking at him hard enough.

"Look, if you're right and Hank was here waiting for us to leave the girls while we chased down a wild goose chase, then he's going to know at this point that we haven't left…"

"So what are you thinking?"

"I'm thinking I need to ensure that Bennet makes it to the police station with that box and Karl in one piece."

"You don't really believe he'd make a move on a cop do you?"

Aaron shrugged, the nagging feeling in his gut hadn't gone anywhere, if anything it had grown. He'd sworn to himself that he would never ignore a feeling like that ever again and he meant to keep the promise. Hank was his problem, his responsibility and if he didn't stop him then there was no one else who could.

"I need you to keep the girls safe while I do this. If I'm wrong then no harm no foul but if I'm not…"

"Aaron, you can't go on your own, if you're right then you'll be placing yourself directly in Hank's way. He doesn't want to get caught…"

Aaron shook his head and started towards the small sports car parked to one side of the drive.

"Hank doesn't want to hurt me, not yet anyway he's too invested in the game. If I can put a stop to the game now then I can put a stop to the loss of life."

Aaron pulled the car door open as Heather appeared out on the porch.

"Aaron!"

She called out to him but he didn't answer her. There was nothing he could say and if he explained to her what he planned on doing then she would only try and stop him. Aaron didn't have time to argue with her. He understood her drive to protect him, to try and keep him safe no matter what because it was the same drive he had over her. He would do anything to keep her and Arianna safe. This was his fault and he had to fix it, if he could prevent Hank from dragging Heather any further into it then he would do it.

Heather's face changed as she watched him climb into the car and she started down the steps, Aaron had just enough time to gun the engine and let the car pounce forward, the wheels spinning until they caught on the drive and the car lunged forward. He pushed the car forward, adjusting the rearview mirror so that the last thing he saw as he pulled out of the drive was Heather.

Chapter Six

THERE HAD BEEN SOMETHING IN the way Aaron had been holding his body as he spoke to David outside. The tension that raced through his body was different and from the moment I'd seen him square his shoulders I'd known I needed to go to him.

Of course, the officers in the hall had tried to stop me and I'd made it outside in time to watch him hop into his car. The look he'd given me was a replica of the look he'd shot me in the hall. Guilt, unspoken apologies, and so much more that I didn't understand. There was a time when he would have explained to me but ever since the situation with Hank had blown up he'd changed. I'd been forced to stand by and watch him grow more and more secretive. Every question I asked him only seemed to make him retreat further into himself.

How was I supposed to help when he wouldn't let me in?

"David, where's he gone? I don't understand why he wouldn't tell me?"

David moved across the drive, each stride purposeful and determined. The look in his eyes made me nervous. He and David had obviously figured something out, something that made the situation a hell of a lot worse, bad enough to send Aaron speeding off into the night.

"Don't you lie to me, David. I don't need sugar coated lies, not from you. You know how I feel about him, you know how worried I am."

"I have to show you something to show you."

David smiled but there was tightness around his eyes that told me the expression was a lie.

I followed him down the steps and out into the middle of the drive. The crackle of police radios and the flash of the lights cast everything in a weird sickly glow.

"Just tell me."

He nodded and turned away from the house. I faced him, folding my arms across my chest as I waited for him to explain to me why my husband had driven into the night as though everyone's life depended on it.

"They've found some listening devices. Well they've found one."

"What do you mean, where?"

I glanced back at the house, my eyes going wide with surprise. How could Hank have gotten any devices near the house? I was almost certain that, that was exactly the sort of thing Aaron had his men sweep for on a regular basis. It seemed impossible to imagine that Hank had planted anything and Aaron's men didn't know about it.

"They know about one around the door where Karl left the box."

"So Karl left the device?"

David shook his head.

"Aaron doesn't seem to think so. He believes that Hank has done it all on purpose, that the cops will only find what he wants them to find. It's more likely that Hank wanted to listen in on what Aaron planned on doing with Karl. It's probably just his way of trying to get ahead once more."

"Can he do that? Do you think he knows how to play Aaron?"

I couldn't keep the fear from my voice. The man I loved was putting himself in the way of a mad man. I didn't know much about Hank but I knew from Aaron's reaction to him that he was bad news. And of course the heart in the box... That only helped to cement my belief that I was right in thinking that Hank was extremely dangerous. But how was I supposed to help Aaron past that? How was I supposed to show him that sharing all of this with me was the way to defeat the man that was tormenting him?

David shrugged and it only made me want to grab him and shake him. He seemed so calm about the entire situation. How could he be so unruffled? Did he not understand? It didn't seem likely that David was oblivious to what Hank was. In fact if anyone was going to know and understand Hank then it would be David. He was Aaron's brother and I knew that David had never trusted the other man. He'd never made his dislike of Hank a secret.

"David, what are holding back from me?"

Realisation hit me. The only way David would be so calm was if he was doing his best to cover something up. He wasn't an actor, and I knew he tended to wear his emotions on his face, much like Aaron did. The only reason he would be this calm was if he was making a conscious effort to keep something from me.

"Nothing, I'm telling you everything I know."

"Then why do I get the feeling that there's more to all of this than you are letting on? Please, David, I asked you not to lie to me. If there is something wrong, something I should know about then please tell me. If it was you and Carrie was hiding something, wouldn't you want me to tell you?"

David dropped his gaze to the ground. I could see from the way his shoulders tightened that I had hit on something. All I needed to do now was press my advantage. He loved Carrie, as much as I loved Aaron, and he knew how hard it was to watch the one you loved keep secrets from you.

"Please, David, tell me. If anything happens to him…"

"Aaron, will be fine, Heather, you need to trust him, he knows how to look after himself."

Groaning with frustration I pushed my hands back through my curly hair.

"I don't doubt Aaron, that isn't where my concern is coming from, David, and you know it. It's Hank I'm concerned about. Aaron might be capable but Hank was his friend."

David lifted his gaze back to mine but I could see from the look in his eyes that he wasn't understanding my point.

"Don't you see? Aaron is a noble man, Hank isn't. The heart that he sent us proves that. If Aaron goes up against him he won't be able to look past the fact that Hank is his friend... If he hesitates, David, for even a moment..."

I cut myself off, David's eyes lighting with fear as it suddenly dawned on him. I was right and I knew it. Aaron was capable, I knew he was strong and there really was no one better at fighting or surviving but where Hank was concerned Aaron seemed to have a blind spot. That blind spot had already caused him guilt over Kirsty. I knew Aaron carried her abduction, almost as though he was the one who had done it. If it was proven that the heart in the box was hers... I wasn't sure how Aaron would carry that.

"He's gone after Bennet, he's worried about him. Aaron thinks Hank might make a move against them, get Karl back... I don't really know if I'm honest but I know I trust Aaron's instincts. If he thinks Hank plans on making some sort of move tonight then he will."

"And you let him go alone?"

Anger ripped through me and it almost stole my breath. I had the sudden urge to let my curled fists show David exactly what I was feeling but it would be a pointless exercise.

"I didn't have a choice, Heather, he made me swear that I would protect you, Arianna, Carrie. We didn't know if Hank would go after Bennet or if he thought he could get at you…"

I didn't wait for David to finish, my feet carrying me to the parking garage at the side of the house. I wasn't about to let Aaron go out into the night on his own, not when Hank was potentially waiting for him out there.

"Heather, you can't go after him. There's nothing you can do…"

"I can help him. If Hank doesn't make a move then I'll have been paranoid for no reason just like Aaron. But if something happens and I could have done something to prevent it…"

I shook my head and fumbled in my pocket for the keycard I knew I would find there. Aaron had rigged most of the exterior exits with an electronic system, I didn't really understand it but I was grateful for it.

With the push of a button the garage door started to slide open, revealing the cars parked within.

David's hand closed around my arm and I fought against his hold.

"Heather, I can't let you go. If I do, he'll kill me."

"And if you don't I'll never forgive you. Even if nothing happens out there, I'll never forgive you."

Gritting my teeth I faced the man I considered to be a brother. It didn't matter what he wanted, I was getting in one of the cars and I was going after my husband.

He studied my face for a moment before releasing me. I saw the look of resignation in his eyes and then something changed. The police officers milling around all seemed to suddenly have a purpose. I watched them head for their cars, the sound of their sirens suddenly ripping the silent night air.

My stomach dropped into my shoes, the air disappearing from my lungs rendering me speechless.

"What's going on?"

David barked at one of the uniformed officers who ran past in the direction of his car. The officer ignored him and kept on running. I knew what was wrong, I could feel it inside like a gaping wound that had just opened up. The moment David's attention was off me I turned and made a dash for the nearest car. I didn't need to sit around and wait for the news I knew was coming.

David's voice rang in my ears as I slammed the locks down on the doors and flipped the ignition on. His face was contorted in anger but there was something else that lurked in his eyes and if I didn't know any better I might have said it was panic.

"Heather, open the door! You can't go after him."

I didn't listen to him, inching the car out of the garage as carefully as I could. I didn't want to hurt him but there was nothing he could do to stop me.

The moment I was in the open I gunned the engine, allowing the car to surge forward. David held onto the door, the noise of his fist slamming against the glass muffled inside the car.

There was a split second of indecision as I watched him run alongside the car. If he didn't let go he was going to end up hurt and that wasn't what I wanted. David came to same conclusion as me, his grip on the door releasing.

I jumped in the driver's seat as he slammed his hands against the top of the car as it passed him, leaving him to stand alone in the now quiet and dark driveway.

There wasn't time to feel guilty. I knew he was doing his best to keep me safe, that he had promised Aaron to look after me but that wasn't Aaron's decision to make. The sooner he realised that I was in it with him the easier it would be on everyone involved.

The road was dark and speed made it difficult to keep the car on the road when navigating the narrow bends. Ahead I could see the flash of police cars, their lights casting strange shapes and shadows on the encroaching trees.

In my mind there was only one thing I was certain of. I had to find Aaron, I had to know he was safe. And yet in my heart I knew there was something terribly wrong. If someone asked me to explain it, then I wouldn't have been able to, it wasn't something that could be explained.

Rounding another bend I slammed on the brakes. Police officers were marking off the road and just beyond them in the dark I could make out curls of smoke lifting into the air.

Killing the engine, I didn't even take the keys from the ignition, leaving them swinging in the dark as I hopped out of the car.

"What happened?"

I ran towards one of the officers who was busy securing the scene.

"Miss, you need to stay behind the barrier."

He lifted his hands indicating the yellow tape blocking the road. I tried to dodge past it but strong arms caught me, pushing me back.

"Is Aaron Ashcroft here?"

My voice lifted in panic, I couldn't help it. I wanted to remain calm, they wouldn't tell me anything if to them I was nothing more than a hysterical woman. But I wasn't calm, I was anything but calm and the harder I tried to pretend the more it seemed to slip away from me.

The officer seemed to hesitate at the mention of Aaron's name.

"Is he alright, please, I just need to know he's alright."

I grabbed the front of his jacket, staring up into his dark eyes as I pleaded with him. I could feel my heart hammering inside my throat and my head was pounding. If he was hurt... If Hank had hurt him...

The cops grip slipped and I jerked past him, my feet slapping across the slick ground. My head refused to understand why the ground was wet, why would it need to be wet when there hadn't been any rain.

I came to a shuddering halt the moment I saw it. There was a scream inside me and it refused to come out. My eyes raked over the mangled remains of Aaron's sports car. I knew it was his, I'd watched him leave in it but now it resembled a crumpled can instead of a car.

No one could have survived that. It didn't seem possible. There was smoke curling up from the broken remains of the car and suddenly it made sense. The car had been on fire. Not only was it completely mangled but it had been on fire.

The ground came up to meet me, the rough surface biting into my hands as I dug my fingers in against the wet asphalt. It was the only thing I could do. It was the only thing that stopped me from completely falling apart. There were no words inside me, nothing, it was like a giant hand had reached inside me and scooped out my insides, everything that made me human was gone and I had no idea what I was supposed to do.

He was gone.

Aaron was gone.

A shout went up from the officers who were up a little further on the road. Through my blurred vision I could see them gathered around the crumpled shell of another car. The sound of screeching metal filled the air. I could hear it grinding and tearing before there was one final crunch and then silence.

I moved on autopilot, pushing up onto my feet and stumbling towards the grouped cops. Pushing through them I watched as they lifted a figure carefully from the car, sliding him up onto a stretcher before they secured him in place.

I wanted it so desperately to be Aaron but as soon as I pushed closer I knew it wasn't him.

Detective Bennet lay on the stretcher, his face masked in blood.

"Aaron."

I didn't even realise I'd said his name aloud until the officers turned to me.

"What the hell is she doing here? Who is she? Get her out of here."

Bennet groaned as they started to wheel him past me, his hand caught mine halting everyone's movement.

"Where is he?"

The words left me in a whisper but despite the noise surrounding us I knew Bennet heard me. His eyes flickered to mine, recognition lighting inside.

"He saved me, if he hadn't intervened I'd be dead."

Bennet's words were quiet and wheezy as though air was getting in somewhere it shouldn't.

"But where is he?"

Bennet tried to shake his head but his movement was restricted by the neck brace and straps that pinned him in place to the backboard.

"He took him…"

I didn't have the chance to ask Bennet who 'he' was but I didn't need to, I already knew the answer to that question.

Chapter Seven

*T*HE ROAD WAS QUIET AS Aaron manoeuvred the car around each bend. He was beginning to wonder if perhaps he had been wrong. Maybe he was being paranoid and there was nothing else going to happen. Hank didn't need to make another move today anyway, he'd already done enough damage.

Light danced against the trees and Aaron slowed his car to little more than a crawl. His heart slowed in his chest, his hands gripping the steering wheel as he killed the engine and let the car roll slowly forward on the natural downward incline.

There was no other cars on the road and the headlights he had seen hadn't been right.

Aaron angled the car, allowing it to curl around the bend providing him with enough of a view.

Bennet's car sat sideways against the barrier that lined the road. One side of the car was completely destroyed as though it had been hit at speed by a train. Of course the only reason Aaron could see all of this was because of the high beams that were trained on the car.

The headlights from the large off road vehicle illuminated most of the road along with the car. Aaron could just make out the slumped form of someone over the steering wheel, from this distance he could only assume it was Bennet.

Hank moved at the back of Bennet's car. Aaron watched as he dragged the unmoving body of Karl from the car. It was impossible to tell if he was alive or dead. Even if he was alive, Aaron didn't like to bet on Karl's survival at the hands of Hank. If David had been right and the plan had been to lure them away from the house all along, then Karl had failed miserably and Aaron knew from experience that Hank didn't like failure.

Pulling his gun from the glove compartment Aaron pushed the car door open as silently as it would allow. Hank had disappeared in behind his own truck making it impossible for Aaron to get a clear shot at him.

"I did wonder if you'd follow Bennet out here."

Hank's voice rang out across the space between them. His words bounced off the trees making it impossible for Aaron to pin point where he stood.

"You know me, Hank, I will always track you down."

LOVING THE BILLIONAIRE EVER AFTER

Aaron fought to keep his voice as level as possible as he moved a little closer to his own car, keeping the metal shape between him and whatever Hank was armed with.

"You always thought you were better than me and I couldn't ever figure out why. How long have you known about me, Aaron? How long have you kept my secret?"

A shudder of revulsion raced through Aaron and he couldn't stop it. In a way Hank was right, if he was honest then he had known what Hank was for longer than he cared to admit. This was a man he had considered a friend, someone he had called in to help him when he knew Heather was in trouble.

Of course Aaron had called Hank in for a reason. He knew what he was capable of, in a tight spot Hank was a powerful weapon, one that if aimed at the right enemy was the perfect soldier. But they weren't at war now, and Hank seemed to see everyone around him as an enemy...

Or did he? Was it just pretence? Maybe Hank honestly just enjoyed inflicting pain on others.

"I never kept your secret, Hank. I thought we were on the same side, I thought we were like brothers, that no matter what happened we could always count on one another."

Hank's laughter rippled through the air but it seemed to be more contained than it had been.

"I was never your brother, Aaron, you have only one of those. We are more alike than you are to him. You and I share more than you will ever share with him. One day you'll realise that and when you do, then I'll be your brother."

The sound of Hank's engine flaring to life burned in Aaron's ears. His headlights swung wildly momentarily blinding Aaron. Aaron slid into the driver's seat of his own car, preparing to follow Hank. A moment passed, little more than a heartbeat of time and Aaron suddenly realised Hank's headlights were growing larger, closer.

There was a moment of silence as Aaron gunned his engine and kicked his car into reverse but it was too late. He had a second to make his decision and as he spun the steering wheel, turning the car away from Hank's oncoming assault Aaron threw himself from the moving car.

The sound of screaming metal filled his ears as he hit the road and curled his body into a tight ball. He rolled across the hard ground, every inch of him aching with the shock of hitting the road.

There was a squeal of tyres as Aaron pushed himself to his feet and staggered towards the edge of the road. He knew Hank was coming for him before he even saw the car.

Aaron pushed his body harder, forcing himself to make it to the side of the road before Hank could mow him down where he stood. He reached the barrier as the edge of Hank's car clipped him, sending him plunging head first into the blackness that lined the edges of the road.

Pain ripped through him as he floated in and out of the darkness that was desperate to claim him. He struggled to grab onto the little flashes of reality that struggled to filter into him.

Pain sparked along his ribs as he tried to move but it was enough to force back the darkness that played along the edges of his vision. All he had to do was hold onto the pain he was feeling, he could use it as a weapon, it would make him stronger.

"Aaron Ashcroft…"

The sound of his name being called by her almost sent him spiralling back down into the darkness. She was back at the house so it was impossible that he could hear her calling for him. Had he imagined it? Was he really that far gone that he was no hallucinating? As far as hallucinations went, hearing Heather calling to him wasn't bad.

One moment seemed to blur into the next and it wasn't until the grinding sound of metal filled the air that Aaron tried to pull himself together. His body was one giant ache but it was the throbbing in his head that hurt the worst. Lifting his hand slowly and unsteadily he pressed it to his head.

One side of his face was covered in something dark and sticky but where he was lying was too dark to make out what it was. He lifted his other arm, relieved to find it working. He shuffled his legs, his ribs protesting as he rolled over onto his side. Each breath he took was like having someone set fire to his lungs.

He groaned as he pushed his body upright, digging his fingers into the walls of the rocky embankment that stretched above him. His body was in no mood for cooperation but Aaron knew he didn't have a choice but to get back up to the road. If he didn't then it was down to whatever rescue services were up there to discover him.

Aaron shivered and pushed his body up, forcing himself to climb the embankment. With each shuddering move he made his ribs screamed in agony, a white hot pain that threatened to send him tumbling back down to the bottom of the ditch he found himself in.

In his head there was only one thing he was certain of and that was that no matter what happened he would get back to Heather. He would find a way to climb out of the ditch and even if he had to crawl on his hands and knees he would get back to her.

It was the only thing that allowed him to keep on pushing, the only thing that forced him to take every painful step upwards.

His hand closed around the top of the embankment, stones and bits of grass coming away in his hand as he fought for purchase. There was shouting and strong arms wrapped around him. Aaron gritted his teeth in an attempt to hold back the moan of pain that fought to escape. His body protested the new pain as he was dragged up and over the edge of the embankment.

He closed his eyes, his lungs burning with each breath he took and then he heard it again.

"Aaron!"

Her frightened scream filled his head and he fought to sit upright against the arms that wanted to hold him down on the stretcher they had placed him on.

"Heather?"

He called out, his mind spinning with possibilities, it was a trick, it had to be a trick, it wasn't possible that she was here with him. She was at home, safe where he left her. David had promised to keep her and Arianna safe. If Heather was truly here then something had happened, something terrible and not worth thinking about.

Of course there was also the possibility that he was simply losing his mind. That the combination of the pain and the constant paranoia had sent him over the edge and he was hallucinating. Neither option was particularly appealing.

Heather's face appeared over his and for a moment Aaron stared at her. He drank her in, the look on her face, the love in her eyes. Of course that love was mixed with other emotions but for a moment Aaron allowed himself the chance to believe that love was all he could see in her face.

Without thinking he lifted his hand to her, his fingers stroking across her soft damp cheek. She clutched at his hand, her fingers closing around his in a vice like grip.

"He had you… I thought he had taken you."

Her voice was choked and broken. Hearing the anguish in her voice was almost enough to push Aaron over the edge. He struggled against the straps that they had pinned him to the gurney with. In that moment there was only one thing he wanted to do and that was hold Heather.

Despite everything she had come looking for him. Their connection was so deeply ingrained within them both that Aaron knew she felt what he felt. There wasn't a mark on her and yet she was just as battered and bruised emotionally as he was physically. It should have been impossible and to try and explain it to someone who'd never experienced a love that strong would be pointless.

The top strap gave beneath his constant pulling and pushing at it and Aaron struggled into an upright position. His body screamed in protest but in that moment he didn't care.

"I'm right here, I'll always be right here."

Drawing her in against his chest, Aaron held her. Heather sobbed against his body, her hands wrapping around his shoulders as she clung to him. The feel of her against him helped. It pushed back the fear that had threatened to eat him in the dark. With Heather in his arms, Aaron suddenly felt invincible, that no matter what Hank threw at him he could overcome it as long as he had her at his side.

"We need to get you down the hospital, have you checked over."

Aaron reluctantly found himself releasing Heather from his tight grip. The pain in his lungs felt worse and he knew the paramedic that stood over him was right. And yet he desperately didn't want to let her go.

As though they'd read his mind the paramedic quickly added.

"She can come with us."

It was like a weight had been lifted from his shoulders as Aaron nodded and settled back against the gurney. It was stupid to think like that but he couldn't help it. He knew there was still so much left to do where Hank was concerned. He couldn't be allowed to get away with the things he was doing. He had to be stopped and deep down Aaron knew he was the only one who could do it. And yet there was a sense of relief that he hadn't had before.

They lifted him into the back of the ambulance and Heather's hand found his. It wasn't until her fingers closed around his that Aaron finally gave himself over to the pain he felt. The last thing he was aware of as the burning in his lungs increased was the press of Heather's hand on his as she sat next to him.

Chapter Eight

*I*T WAS THE LONGEST NIGHT of my life as I sat and waited for the doctor's to give me news on Aaron. He'd been awake when they'd lifted him from the edge of the embankment and looking at the state of his car everyone was amazed by his survival.

When he'd wrapped his arms around my shoulders and held me I'd managed to convince myself that he wasn't that hurt. That the blood on his face and the bruising down the side of his body was simply superficial. And then it had all changed.

Watching him slip away from me in the back of the ambulance had almost crippled me. I'd never been more helpless in all my life as they fought to bring his blood pressure and heart rate back up.

I wanted to grab him, shake him until he looked up at me with that lazy teasing smile of his that I'd come to cherish. The thought that I might never get that again had crushed my own heart in my chest.

I still couldn't understand how he'd been so alert and then...

David sat at the other end of the waiting area, Carrie at his side as she struggled to console him. The only thing I was glad about was that Arianna wasn't old enough to understand what was going on.

"Mrs Ashcroft?"

One of the doctors tapped my shoulder and leaned down towards me. I jumped, my thoughts scattering to the winds as I stood.

"What's happened, how is he?"

"Surprisingly, he's ok, a few broken ribs, some concussion and other bumps and bruises. Other than that he's fine."

"But he crashed in the ambulance? How can he be fine?"

The doctor smiled sympathetically.

"One of his ribs was putting pressure on his lungs, the break meant they were being compressed. We've since then stabilised it and reduced the pressure. The combination of that with the shock was responsible for his drop in blood pressure."

I dropped back against the seat, the air leaving my body in one long whoosh. For one whole minute my body had no idea what it was supposed to do. I wanted to run up and down the hall screaming with happiness but I was tired and it wasn't just a physical tiredness anymore. I was emotionally exhausted. After everything we'd been through this time seemed too close. Part of me couldn't help but wonder had I been a terrible person in a previous life or something because the constant threat of losing the man I loved was a punishment.

"Mrs Ashcroft, are you alright?"

The doctor leaned down towards me, crouching next to the chair I sat in he watched me carefully. I had the sudden urge to laugh, the sound escaped me in a sudden burst and within seconds the laughter had turned to sobs.

Carrie wrapped her arms around me, drawing me in against her body as she rocked me back and forth.

"Heather, what's wrong? Aaron is going to be fine."

"I know that but I could have lost him… What if I had lost him? What am I supposed to do without him?"

"But you're not without him, you don't have to do anything without him. The doctor is going to let you in to see him when you're feeling better."

I sat up and scrubbed my hands back across my face. I felt like such a fool breaking down in tears after hearing that Aaron would be fine. How was I supposed to explain the feeling I had?

"I thought with Jude gone that things would start to fall into place. I thought we would have time to enjoy our life together, instead of constantly looking over our shoulders."

"And you will have that, I know you will. Heather, you've got so much to be happy about, so much joy in your life."

"And heartache… There's always something. What happens when we don't win? What happens if Hank wins? He sent a heart in a box, he's not exactly someone to be messed with. What happens if he gets the better of Aaron?"

Carrie sat back against the plastic seats. I could see the utter conviction in her eyes. She believed in David and Aaron completely and so did I. But I also couldn't live my life looking through rose tinted glasses. Aaron wasn't super human, at the end of the day he was a man just like any other and what I had witnessed in the ambulance had more than proven that to me.

I'd come so close to losing him and it was more than I could bear.

"I think you need to see him, Heather. Aaron is strong, you need to trust that he's stronger than Hank."

David's words surprised me, he spoke as though he knew exactly what I was thinking. I hadn't truly shared what was in my head so it was impossible to believe that he knew what I thought but as I looked up into his face I realised he knew more than he was letting on.

"You're probably right."

David nodded and the look in his eyes told me he understood.

Pushing away from the seats I stood and moved down the hall after the doctor.

"How soon can I see him, Doctor?"

"As soon as you like, he's a very resilient man, I think you'll be pleasantly surprised."

I smiled politely but as hard as I tried I still couldn't shake the image of Aaron lying flat out on the stretcher. The way his hand had slipped from mine, the stillness of his body, it was a nightmare come true and it was something I wouldn't get over in a hurry.

I followed the doctor down the long sterile hall. He pushed open a door at the opposite end and stood aside, holding the door so I could move through it.

The light in the room was soft and nothing like the normal harsh fluorescent brilliance I'd come to associate with hospitals.

"You look as bad as I feel."

Aaron's voice drew my attention to the bed. He was sitting up, thick white pillows propped against his back. The ghost of a grin hovered around his lips and I wanted to throw myself across the room to him, catch his face between my hands and kiss his mouth.

"Don't you dare make a joke about all of this."

My voice wobbled as I spoke and I fought to keep my emotions in check. The last thing I wanted to do was break down and turn into a blubbering mess.

"Heather, don't be like that, you know if I could have done it any other way I would have."

"You didn't need to go after him. You could have told the cops about your suspicion… You didn't need to be the one to get hurt."

"I wasn't the only one. Bennet is in a bad way and Karl is gone…"

"I don't care about them, Aaron, I don't care about anyone but you. God why can't you understand that?"

I blew out a frustrated breath and covered my face with my hands. The sound of the bed creaking made me glance up. The covers were flipped back and Aaron was struggling to push himself to his feet.

I went to him, wrapping my arms around him as I tried to stop him from getting to his feet.

"Don't, you're hurt. Why can't you do what the doctors tell you for once in your life?"

He smiled and then winced as he sat back against the pillows once more. The shadow of pain in his eyes was enough to break my heart. I just wanted him safe. We'd lost so much, risked so much already. I couldn't lose him, I wouldn't lose him.

He reached up to me, his hand cupping my cheek gently.

"Heather, look at me."

His voice was soft and it took me a moment to realise that I'd closed my eyes the moment he touched me.

"I can't lose you, Aaron. You can't do that to me."

He cupped my face between his hands, drawing me down to the bed.

"You're not going to lose me, Heather, I'd never leave you. The one thing that pulled me out of that ditch was the thought of getting back to you. It was the only thing that kept me going, kept me moving forward."

I opened my eyes and stared down at him. My vision was blurred with my unshed tears and I tried to blink them away as they started down my cheeks.

He leaned up towards me, his lips brushing against mine, soft, chaste. With a desperate sigh I gave myself over to him, the kiss deepening. Warmth spread through me as I wrapped my arms around his shoulders.

He traced his tongue along the edge of my lips and I opened to him easily. His hands found the back of my neck, his grip strong as he held me to him.

The sound of someone coughing was the only thing that broke us apart. I sprang away from Aaron, a guilty blush spreading up over my face and up into my hairline as I turned to stare at David and Carrie standing in the door.

"We came to see you, but I guess you're completely recovered."

David's tone was dry and sarcastic but I could see the happy glint in his eyes and I knew he was just as relieved to see Aaron sitting up in bed as I was.

"What can I say, it's amazing what the attentions of a beautiful woman can do for my health."

He caught my hand in his and drew me further up the bed towards him and I went with him happily. Aaron's arms were still and always would be the safest place I'd ever been. Of course if didn't change the fact that I would worry and panic about him. It didn't change the fact that I thought his actions from earlier in the evening were needlessly reckless.

David moved into the room and pulled two chairs from the corner of the room, drawing them up to the side of the bed before gesturing to Carrie to sit. She looked exhausted and I could see dark rings beneath her eyes. It seemed just like the rest of us she was suffering from sleepless nights, the only problem was she wasn't just looking after herself anymore.

Watching her carefully I promised myself I would speak to her privately as soon as Aaron and I were home. I'd gone through many of the same things as her and if I could help make it easier for her and the baby then I would do it.

"What did Hank want?"

David's tone was all business as soon as he was seated beside the bed.

Aaron shrugged and then winced once more. I watched him carefully and I knew the pain was exhausting him but he was strong and there was no way he would admit that he was suffering.

"Maybe this is a conversation we could have once everyone has had a goodnights sleep?"

I expected my suggestion to be immediately dismissed but I caught Carrie's eye and she nodded almost imperceptibly. I knew she'd seen the look in Aaron's eyes and if it was David lying in the bed she would have been the first one to order everyone out.

"We need to know what Hank is planning, Heather, he can't be allowed to just get away with whatever in hell he wants." David said leaning forward in his chair.

"I know that but Aaron had been through hell, he needs to get his strength back and discussing it now or in a few hours from now, isn't going to change anything."

Aaron shook his head and opened his mouth to speak. "Heather, I'm fine really, I…"

Carrie wrapped her hand around David's and winced.

"Aaron might be fit to stay up and fight Hank but I'm not."

I tried to hide my grin and the flash in her eyes told me exactly what she was up to.

David's attention instantly snapped to her face, his hand closing around hers as his face was wreathed in concern.

"Carrie, I didn't think, I'm sorry we should get you home."

He stood tugging her to her feet and in against his body. He shot Aaron a sheepish look over his shoulder.

"Sorry, Aaron, I'll come back later but first…"

Aaron cut him off with a smile, his hand momentarily tightening around mine.

"It's fine, you have something far more important to do. You have to look after the woman who is carrying your future."

He grinned and winked at Carrie who simply blushed in response. As she turned for the door she winked at me, it happened so quickly I doubted myself that it had even happened.

The moment they disappeared out through the door silence descended on the room once more.

"Speaking of the future, where's Arianna?"

Aaron winced again and his voice was suddenly filled with a weariness he hadn't shown when David and Carrie had sat with us.

"Mom, took her. I thought at least if she had her she'd be safe."

"Your mother didn't mind taking her?"

I laughed and crawled up beside him, curling my body protectively around his.

"Mind taking her only granddaughter? Are you kidding me? She was thrilled, by the time my mother is finished with spoiling her, Arianna isn't going to want to come home to boring old us."

Aaron smiled but I could tell that he was beginning to slip towards sleep. Dipping my head I pressed my lips to the top of his forehead.

"I'll let you get some sleep."

His hand suddenly tightened on mine once more.

"Stay with me, just like you are… Please?"

I swallowed back the lump that suddenly appeared in my throat. It seemed I wasn't the only one who understood how close it had come. I didn't say anything, there was no point not now. The only thing I could do now was hold him as he slept and pray that tomorrow would bring at least some good news.

Chapter Nine

*S*TANDING IN FRONT OF THE small bathroom mirror Aaron winced. His ribs ached like the devil himself had broken them and the time spent in the hospital had been less than comfortable. Of course if Aaron had been allowed to get his own way he wouldn't have spent any time in the hospital beyond the first night. Lying in a bed wasn't going to see Hank caught.

"Mr Ashcroft, I really do recommend that you reconsider what you're doing. You're in no fit state to leave."

Aaron shook his head and fastened the last button on his shirt. The doctors had spent most of the morning trying to convince him of how foolish his actions were. The more they tried to tell him he was wrong, the more convinced Aaron became of his decision.

"If I stay in here much longer I'll go mad. I'm not the type of man to lie in bed and recover, it takes too long."

"But leaving too soon might do more harm than good."

Aaron sighed and leaned on the edge of the sink. There had to be a way to make them understand that he simply wasn't interested in their concerns. Aaron knew his own body, he knew how it worked and how far he could afford to push it before things became too dangerous. He was sore but he wasn't broken and he wasn't about to let a few broken ribs stop him from doing what needed to be done.

"Look, I know you mean well."

Aaron leaned against the door jamb as he spoke, his fingers deftly fastening the small buttons on the cuff of his shirt.

"I don't just mean well, Mr Ashcroft, it's my job to determine when you're fit to be discharged and I just don't think you're ready."

"So I'll sign myself out. The only certainty, Doc, is that I'm leaving."

The doctor sighed and Aaron could see that he was clearly frustrated. He wanted to feel guilty but he just couldn't bring himself to feel it. He knew the doctor was just doing his job but as far as Aaron could see he was just standing in the way of progress. There was too much at stake and Aaron would have been happier with someone who wanted to help him and not hinder him by trying to make out that he was sicker than he actually was.

"You're a stubborn man, Mr Ashcroft, I just hope that doesn't get you in trouble."

The doctor stood and headed for the door, Aaron watched him carefully half expecting him to turn around and ask him once more to stay. He didn't and Aaron let out a sigh of relief as he pulled the door shut behind him.

Heading for the bed Aaron scooped the cell phone up from its place on the bed. He'd already called ahead for a car. He might be prepared to argue with everyone else about his ability to check out of the hospital but he really didn't want to drive. The thought of wrenching a wheel back and forth as he navigated the hair pin bends on the road back to the house made his already sore ribs ache more.

He pushed the phone into the inside pocket of his jacket before tugging it on. He couldn't help but wince as the pain flared through him. Sucking in a deep breath Aaron let the pain wash over him. Pain was something he could use, Hank had done this to him and as far as Aaron was concerned it was high time he repaid the favour.

Sitting in the back of the car Aaron stared out the window at the scenery that flashed by. Heather had already called his cell phone twice and both calls he had sent straight to his messaging service. The thought of explaining to her why he wasn't in the hospital wasn't particularly appealing. Turning up on the doorstep somehow seemed like a much better idea.

The car rolled into the drive and Aaron's mind flipped back to the last time he had been in the driveway. The cop cars that had covered every inch of space, Aaron could make out the tyre tracks that covered parts of the lawn where the drive hadn't been big enough. Closing his eyes he could practically see the red and blue flash of lights that had lit everything up.

He shook his head as the car rolled to a stop. Aaron didn't have a chance to reach for the door, as soon as the car stopped it was wrenched open and Heather poked her head inside.

"What the hell are you doing here? I didn't think they wanted to let you go?"

Aaron smiled and slid across the seat towards her. She backed out into the watery sunshine as he stepped out of the car and stood in front of her.

"They let me out for good behaviour."

Aaron grinned and wrapped her into his arms. She went to him willingly, her arms automatically closing around his waist. She peered up at him, her red hair falling across her face.

"But they didn't think you were ready to leave yesterday, I asked the nurses and they seemed to think it would be another few days…"

Heather paused her eyes narrowing suspiciously.

"You discharged yourself didn't you?"

He could hear the hum of anger in her voice and the last thing he wanted was to make her angrier. All Aaron wanted to do was hold her in his arms, kiss her until she gave into him and retired to bed with him.

"No they let me out. The doctor was very impressed with me when he did his rounds this morning. I asked him if I could go home and recuperate there and he seemed to think it was a great idea."

The suspicious look on Heather's face didn't leave and Aaron knew she was trying to read him. She was extremely perceptive and one false move on his behalf and she would know that he was lying.

"Aaron, why can't you just do as they ask for once?"

She sighed and pulled out of his grip as she folded her arms across her chest.

"If it was me and I discharged myself from the hospital you'd have a fit."

Aaron pulled his gaze away from her face and pushed the car door shut. She was right and he was probably a hypocrite to think it but he couldn't help it. Heather was precious to him and he would do anything to keep her and their child safe, including leaving hospital against the doctors wishes.

"None of it matters now anyway, I'm home and I'm not going back, there's too much to do."

Aaron tried to keep his voice as even as he could. He didn't want to start a fight, he already knew how determined and stubborn Heather could be. To give her the opportunity to really dig her heels in about something would be the worst thing he could possibly do.

"Is David here?"

Aaron chose to change the subject, it seemed like the only way to avoid an argument. Aaron had never seen Heather so upset about this type of situation before. Even when Jude had terrorised her she hadn't seemed as angry and scared as she was now. None of it made sense and she didn't seem to be in any hurry to share her thoughts about the situation with him. Perhaps it was something she would never want to share with him, all Aaron could hope for was that by taking Hank out of the picture she might relax a little more than she was.

"He's in the study." She paused for a moment and then moved in against him. She wrapped her arms around his body before he had the chance to focus in on her face or prepare for what she was about to do.

"You had me so worried. Don't you ever do it to me again, do you hear me? I won't lose you, Aaron."

He wrapped his body around her, holding her tightly to his body.

"I've already told you, Heather, you don't have to worry. I'm not going anywhere. It would take a hell of a lot more to take me from you and Arianna."

"I can't help but think that maybe Hank is more than we bargained for. I know he was your friend but you obviously didn't know him, you obviously didn't know what he was capable of."

Her words froze Aaron in place. His heart faltered and stopped and his breath seemed to catch in his lungs. She was wrong, deep down he had known what Hank was, he had to have known and yet for so long he ignored it because it didn't fit in with his plans. How could he tell her that she was in love with a man just as bad as Hank, maybe even worse?

Heather wouldn't want to stay with him if she knew the truth. If she knew what he was truly capable of there would be no way that she would want to know him, let alone love him. If she found out the truth he would lose everything, her, Arianna, his reason for existing. But he loved her so how was he supposed to keep a secret like that from her? It didn't seem fair.

"Aaron, are you alright?"

Heather's worried voice cut through his thoughts and drew him back to the moment. He still stood with his arms wrapped around her but she had taken a small step back in order to look up into his face. The concern in her eyes was very real but if she knew the truth it wouldn't be concern that he would see in her eyes.

"I'm fine, I'm just tired, there's a lot to get sorted."

He smiled at her, or at least as close to a smile as he could get without forcing it too much and making it false.

She watched him for a moment before she nodded.

"Just promise me you'll look after yourself?"

Aaron grinned and this time it was genuine. She was truly the most amazing woman he had ever met and there wasn't a day that went by when he didn't question how he'd been lucky enough to draw her eye. She was perfect in every way and the more time he spent with her the less he wanted to ever be away from her.

He didn't answer her, choosing to tug her against his body, hard enough to knock the air from her lungs. He dipped his face to hers, his tongue sliding along her lips as his mouth closed over hers.

She tasted of strawberries and other sweet things that he couldn't quite put his finger on. Closing his eyes, Aaron pulled her further into his body, deepening the kiss until Heather moaned softly against his mouth.

The sound of her soft cry of desire only made him long for more. Without thinking about what he was doing, he spun her around, his ribs protesting wildly as he pinned her against the side of the car. His hands wandered down over her body grazing the sides of her breasts through the soft jumper she wore.

He pushed his knee between her legs forcing them apart as he nibbled along the soft curve of her bottom lip. Heather gasped, her head falling back as Aaron moved from her mouth, his lips dropping passionate kisses along the soft column of her neck.

There was something so addictive about Heather. The moment he tasted her he always wanted more and no matter how many times he sated himself inside her it was never enough.

He reached the neckline of her jumper and stopped. For a moment he contemplated stripping her then and there, taking what was his against the side of the car. Heather moaned against him, bucking her hips against him, grinding her body down on the leg he thrust between her thighs.

"Not here, Heather, what's mine stays mine and I don't want an audience."

He whispered his words against her ear and Heather whimpered. She slowly opened her eyes, her pupils dilated with lust and her cheeks flushed with colour.

It suddenly seemed to dawn on her that they weren't alone. Aaron knew the guards were there, watching them. Of course if he had turned and glanced up at them they would appear as though they were completely oblivious to what was going on. But Aaron could feel their eyes on him, their gazes hungry as they watched him ravish his wife against the car.

"Oh, God, who saw us?"

Heather suddenly seemed to realise what he meant, the flush in her cheeks suddenly deepening as it spread up into her hairline. She chewed her lips, lips that just moments before he had bitten down on. They were flooded with colour, instead of their usual soft rose colour they were now a vibrant red. A sign that she was thoroughly kissed.

Aaron had the sudden urge to kiss her again, to draw her bottom lip out between his teeth, to bite down on it until she whimpered for mercy.

Instead, he fought the urge a smile curling his lips.

"Everyone is more than aware of what we get up to."

"But normally it happens behind closed doors."

Heather fought to cover her face with her hands but Aaron held her still and dipped his face until he could trail his lips across her neck.

"Aaron, don't, please."

But she wasn't entirely serious, the giggling that erupted from her when his breath tickled across her soft skin gave her away.

He pulled away from her and stared down at her, a wave of emotion suddenly swamping him.

"I love you, Heather, I don't think I ever believed I'd ever be this happy."

She shook her head the smile fading on her face.

"Neither did I. I believed for so long that I would never have peace and happiness seemed utterly out of the question. All of this," she gestured to her surroundings, "all of this seemed completely impossible."

"I know."

Aaron didn't need to say anything else. He knew exactly what she meant, the separation they had suffered at the hands of Jude had been unbearable but he knew she believed it was the only way to keep those she loved safe. Finding her once more had seemed too good to be true and Jude's constant drive to tear them apart had left Aaron with trust issues.

He loved Heather but he constantly lived with the fear that one day he would wake up and she would be gone again. What if they day came when she decided it was all too much... Too dangerous? There was so much to lose now and it left Aaron with a feeling of desperation.

"What are you thinking?"

Heather's voice startled Aaron from his own thoughts and without even thinking about it he plastered a fake smile on his face once more and shook his head.

"Nothing that matters."

He wrapped his arm around her shoulders and started back towards the house.

"Where's Arianna?"

He glanced down at Heather in an attempt to gauge her reaction to his changing of the subject.

"She's not here, I'm waiting for Cynthia and Mom to drop her back. I was going to bring her into the hospital to see you."

"Why is she with your mother?"

Aaron paused on the steps and stared down at Heather.

"I thought it was safer, I told you that…"

"No, you told me the first night that you left her with your mother. You didn't tell me you planned to leave her there indefinitely."

"I didn't leave her there indefinitely, Aaron, what the hell has gotten into you?"

Heather pulled out of his grip and frowned up at him but he could see the uneasiness in her eyes and he knew he had struck on the truth.

"You don't trust me to keep you safe, to keep Arianna safe?"

"Don't be ridiculous…"

Heather's voice trembled.

"I trust you, Aaron, I don't trust anyone else…"

"So without me here you'd rather send Arianna away?"

Heather nodded without answering him. Aaron didn't know what to say, what could he say to her he understood her fear. But it also terrified him to know that she was so afraid. He'd lost her once and he wouldn't do it again.

The front door opened inwards and David appeared on the top step.

"I didn't think you were due back just yet."

Aaron grinned up at his brother and just like that the conversation with Heather was over. It wasn't something he wanted to let go and promised himself that once they had a moment alone he would speak to her. There had to be some way he could reassure her that nothing would ever happen, not now and not as long as he had breath.

Heather smiled at him, following him up into the house before turning and disappearing down towards the kitchen, leaving Aaron with David. He watched her go, his mind whirring with thoughts, the only certainty in his mind was that he wouldn't let her go.

Chapter Ten

I MADE IT INTO THE kitchen before my tears started down my face. They fell hot and heavy and as hard as I tried to brush them away I couldn't. The air caught in my throat as I sobbed. I'd seen the look in Aaron's eyes, recognised it instantly. He didn't trust me, didn't trust that I would stay with him no matter what happened.

He was wrong, utterly and completely wrong. I would always protect Arianna, I would do whatever it took to keep her safe but I would never desert Aaron, not after the last time.

I'd been a coward when Jude had first gotten to me but that was all in the past. Aaron gave me the confidence to believe that I was capable of anything. Together nothing could ever hurt us.

But if he was doubting me then how together were we really?

How could we be strong if there was unspoken tension between us? Why he would doubt me now after everything we had been through left me baffled. I'd never given him any reason to doubt me, not now…

"Heather, are you alright?"

Carrie's soft voice made me jump and I hastily scrubbed at my face.

"I'm fine."

I didn't want to share my feelings, I wasn't sure I even knew how to share my thoughts or what I was feeling. How did you explain a look you saw in someone's eyes? She'd probably just think I was mad, or that I was imagining it and I didn't think I could take it if that was what she thought.

"He'll be fine, he's strong."

"I know he is, I think it's probably just the emotion of everything that's going on…"

Carrie nodded and chewed her lip for a minute before handing over a bundle of letters. It took me a moment to realise it was the mail and the moment I did, I couldn't stop the laughter that erupted from me. I'd become so paranoid about everything that I was even looking at the mail suspiciously, I wasn't sure what exactly I expected it to do to me but it wasn't good.

I dropped the letters on the counter, scooping up the top one that was addressed to me. I ripped it open, my eyes scanning down the page as my heartbeat slowly grew louder in my ears.

"What is it?"

Carrie stepped up beside me and I knew the expression I wore betrayed what I felt.

"It's a letter from the court, they want me to testify against Jude. And they want me to come in for a meeting, to explain what will happen."

"I thought Aaron was trying to keep you out of it?"

I shrugged and stared down at the letter, the words blurring into each other as I reread it over and over.

The last thing I wanted to do was face him in court. The thought of his eyes watching me, the knowing smile I knew he would wear. If I faced him in court it would only be the beginning of the problems he would throw my way.

"He was trying and I guess this proves he can't."

"Can they just do that though? They know what he put you through, surely that counts for something?"

"I don't think it does. I survived him, many women didn't and I suppose they need something concrete to pin on him."

"Heather, they have enough evidence, that case is airtight... All those months while he was in a coma they were building that case."

I dropped the letter onto the counter as the sound of the front doorbell sounded, it's echo rumbling through the house.

"I guess I need to go to the meeting and see what they have in mind… They have something planned, I just don't know what it is."

I moved from the kitchen and down the hall. One of the guards stood at the open door and just beyond him on the doorstep I could see my mother and Cynthia. My heart skipped in my chest as I heard the familiar gurgle of Arianna and I instantly wished she was in my arms.

Being apart from her was hard, practically impossible. There was so much I wanted to protect her from and logically I knew it was safer for her to spend time with my mom but it didn't make me feel any less like I was abandoning her. Life without her was empty and I struggled to control my instincts that screamed to snatch her into my arms.

Cynthia took one look at my face and seemed to instantly know what had happened.

"You got the letter too, didn't you? They want you to testify."

"You got it too?"

She shrugged but there was a tightening around her eyes that was almost imperceptible but I caught it.

"It makes sense. Who else can they get to put him away? Without us there's nothing solid."

I nodded and held my arms out. She passed Arianna back to me without a word and I buried my face in against the fluffy tufts of baby hair on Arianna's head. I breathed in her scent and closed my eyes. I couldn't explain why but holding her in my arms made everything much easier to deal with.

A hand touched my cheek and I opened my eyes. Mom watched me carefully, the look in her eyes soft, as though she expected at any moment that I might break apart. I smiled but it wasn't a happy look.

"You'll get through this, Heather. You both will."

She turned and included Cynthia in her statement. There was a flinching in my sister's eyes and it broke my heart to see it. She had been doing so well, recovering from the trauma she had suffered at the hands of such a complete monster. And all of that seemed to change when Mandy had attacked her.

Cynthia had moved back to live with our mother unable to face what had happened inside her own home. Of course she wouldn't admit to her fear, and her trips to therapy had suddenly stopped too. I was worried about her but each time I tried to broach the subject she instantly pushed me away and behaved as though I was simply pitying her.

"I don't have a problem with testifying, Heather is the one who seems to have an issue."

Cynthia's voice was curt and filled with anger. I wanted to reach out to her, to tell her that everything would be alright but I had done that in the past and I had failed her. I'd promised I would keep her safe from Jude and I'd failed miserably.

"Cynthia, I don't think Heather is concerned about testifying, I think it's because of who you'll both be testifying against."

I shrugged and moved away from the door, gesturing for them to follow me inside. As we passed the door to Aaron's office Cynthia hesitated.

"I thought Aaron wasn't due out for a few days?"

"He wasn't, he discharged himself."

"Is he fit to be out?"

Mom moved past the door and followed me as I headed for the kitchen. Her tone of voice suggested she was actually concerned for him and it surprised me a little.

"He seems to think so and who am I to doubt him. I can't tell how much pain he's in, I can't see his injuries and if the doctor's warnings weren't strong enough to keep him in the hospital then maybe he is fit to be out."

I shifted Arianna in my embrace until she lay against my shoulder.

"And if Hank tries again? What happens then? Isn't he endangering you both by getting out early?"

"I don't think so, we're more vulnerable without Aaron…"

Cynthia cut me off as she dropped down onto one of the kitchen stools and waved her hand in the air.

"Oh come on, Heather, you're not vulnerable without him, he'd do anything to keep you safe. You live in a house loaded to the hilt with guards and security. You're one of the safest people on earth, you always were."

The tone of her voice suggested a bitterness I hadn't expected from her.

"Cynthia, what's your problem?"

I tried to keep my voice devoid of any emotion, I tried to keep the question as simply a question but I couldn't.

"Problem? I don't have a problem, Heather, you're the one with the problem. You're always the one with the problem. It seems every time I turn around you have a new issue in your life."

"Cynthia."

Mom's voice was sharp as she attempted to halt Cynthia's sudden tirade. Maybe she was right. It was beginning to feel as though no matter what happened there was always someone trying to disrupt the little bit of peace I might have found. But I didn't know how to change it and I certainly wasn't trying to bring it on myself. If I had a choice in the matter I would never have asked for any of this.

"No, I won't stop, Mother. Why are you always defending her? She sends Arianna to because she thinks she'll be safer with you but did she even stop to think that maybe she making a target out of you?

"Did it even occur to you that the lunatic that put Aaron in the hospital might target us in an attempt to get to Arianna? We don't have the protection you do, Heather. We're the vulnerable ones."

"Cynthia, you're not vulnerable. Hank doesn't know anything about you. He's not interested in hurting you, neither of you have done anything to him."

"I hadn't done anything to Jude either and that didn't stop him from targeting me to get at you."

"You know I never wanted any of that to happen, Cynthia. I would never have put you in harms way, you have to know that. I never imagined he would do…"

"You never imagined? That's just the point isn't it? You never imagine. You don't think, you just breeze through life and it's always everyone else who ends up caught in the crosshairs. I won't have it happen again, Heather. I won't be abused and hurt because the crap from your life spills out of control and into mine."

She stood suddenly, her chair scrapping back against the floor until it slammed into the wall. Mom stood, holding her hand out to Cynthia, a look of complete shock on her face. Cynthia ignored her, choosing instead to storm from the room, leaving the rest of us to watch after her in silence.

"When did she become so bitter?"

"Don't be so hard on her, Heather, she's had a rough time and she doesn't have someone she can fall back on."

I shook my head not sure how to answer my mother. It was true, Cynthia had a much rougher ride than most her age and I felt for her but there was no point in blaming the people that loved you. If I could have changed the past I would have. Hindsight was always twenty twenty and I had it in spades now.

"I best go after her. When you know more about Hank or the meeting you have to go to with the attorneys then let me know. Maybe it'll help me understand how to help Cynthia."

I nodded but I didn't answer her. She paused and watched me carefully as though unsure if she should continue talking. I knew she was holding something back and a part of me was desperate to know what it was but I held my tongue.

She stroked her hand over Arianna's curly haired head and smiled sadly before turning and following Cynthia from the room.

I loved Cynthia but if she was determined to hate me because of what happened there wasn't much I could do to change her mind. Deep down I couldn't blame her, Jude had wanted me and Cynthia was the one person he knew he could use to get to me. I'd exposed her to a monster and that was something I would have to deal with for the rest of my life.

Chapter Eleven

AARON PACED THE LENGTH OF the office. David was perched on the long couch, his feet propped up on the table and Aaron could feel his eyes following each step he took.

Pacing wasn't helping him to think any better but it certainly seemed like a better idea than sitting and doing nothing.

"They have nothing on him. He left nothing at the scene and Bennet can barely remember what happened."

"Is that man capable of doing anything right? I saved him. Hank wouldn't have left him alive if I hadn't been there to distract him."

Aaron sighed and covered his face with his hands. He winced behind his fingers as his ribs protested fiercely, pain burning along his lungs. There was too much at stake, he didn't have time to be anything but his best right now.

But then that was probably exactly what Hank had hoped for.

Aaron knew that Hank couldn't beat him, not in a fair fight anyway and Hank knew it too. It was the perfect reason to leave him injured but not dead. Hank wanted desperately to win at this game he had set up, the injuries Aaron had sustained was just the beginning of Hank's advantage.

"Bennet is really trying, Aaron, you know that but none of this can be easy for him. Between Jude and now Hank, I don't imagine he's ever dealt with so many dangerous people in such a short time."

"It's not good enough, David, you and I know that. Bennet't best won't be a match for Hank. He needs to let me in on this. I can stop him, I know I can beat him and I'm the only one who can play his game."

David laughed but it wasn't a pleasant sound. Aaron let his furious scowl focus completely on David as he stopped pacing and paused in front of the couch.

"What the hell is that supposed to mean? You don't think I'm right?"

"I think the last time you went up against him you ended up in the hospital. The time before that he helped you get Heather back but she almost died and the time before that…"

David physically shuddered and for the first time in a long time Aaron saw concern in his brother's eyes.

"That was an accident and entirely my fault, he saved my life then."

"That's what you say, Aaron, but you don't remember most of that mission. The shrink said it was some sort of PTSD, that you blocked out the trauma rather than remember what had really happened. Well what if the real trauma was that Hank had betrayed you."

Aaron shook his head but if he was honest he wasn't entirely sure anymore. David was right about one thing and that was that there were too many gaps in the last mission to be certain of anything.

Grabbing the bottle of scotch from the shelf, Aaron scooped two glasses up and carried them over to the sofa where David sat. He dumped both glasses on the table and proceeded to fill them with the warm amber liquid. He didn't wait for David to grab his own glass before he swallowed the contents of his tumbler in one hard gulp.

The alcohol burned down the back of his throat momentarily numbing him to the pain that was doing its best to over ride his senses.

"You don't want to believe it but you have to know it's a possibility."

"Of course I know it's a possibility. You're right, I don't remember enough of what happened on that mission. I keep having dreams about it, like my brain is trying to tell me something, I just don't know what it is."

"What sort of dreams."

David sat back on the couch and swallowed the amber liquid in his glass.

"They're not something I care to talk about, suffice to say they're bad and they're all connected to that mission."

There was a quiet knock on the door and Aaron fell silent. Boris, one of the guards who had been called into the fill the place of the two guards Aaron had fired poked his head in around the door.

"Detective Bennet and two other men are here to see you."

"When did Bennet get out of the hospital?"

Aaron just had enough time to get the question out before Bennet pushed past Boris and strode into the room.

"Before you did."

Bennet said as he limped into the centre of the room. The right side of his face was black and blue and his eye was blood shot. His right arm was in a sling and the white cast that covered his arm seemed to be at odds with the grey suit jacket he was wearing.

"Couldn't have been much sooner than me, you look like a mess."

Aaron added but there was no malice in his tone. The other man did look a mess but it seemed to be more superficial than anything else.

"You're one to talk."

Bennet grinned and moved forward holding his left hand out at an awkward angle.

"I didn't get the chance to thank you. If you hadn't turned up when you did I wouldn't be standing here. He meant to kill me."

"I know."

Aaron took Bennet's extended hand and his eyes flickered to the two other men who had stepped into the room after the Detective. One of them was obviously just another detective. Bennet had probably been forced to take someone else with him now, Aaron couldn't imagine being fit to do much driving with his arm in the cast.

However it was the other man that caught Aaron's eye. Something niggled at him and bile crept up the back of his throat. There was something completely familiar about the man standing in front of him and Aaron hated not being able to put his finger on why.

"Who are your friends?"

Aaron tried to keep the curiosity from his voice but the stranger's eyes immediately flickered to his face, the look in his gaze filling Aaron with unease.

"This is Toby, he's a new detective and he gets the unenviable task of chauffeuring me everywhere."

"With all due respect, Sir, that's not the reason I asked for this assignment."

"Then why did you? And if you tell me once more about how it's a great opportunity to work on such an important case, I'll beat some sense into you with my cast."

Toby instantly fell silent but the look on his face was defiant and Aaron struggled to keep a smile from curling his lips. He could admire Toby's drive to succeed and the cases that Bennet worked on were some of the most prolific the force had dealt with. It made career sense to become Bennet's glorified driver, if it meant getting in on the action at such a young age. The only problem in the entire plan as far as Aaron could see was Hank.

Toby was new and inexperienced and just the type of toy Hank would enjoy ripping apart. He'd always despised new recruits and Aaron knew the perverse pleasure he'd taken in torturing them with cruel pranks when they'd worked together as part of Special Ops.

"And this is Agent McKinley."

The man Bennet had just introduced as McKinley stepped forward and held his hand out to Aaron.

"It's nice to finally put a real face to the reports."

McKinley's words made the hairs on the back of Aaron's neck stand on end. This was no ordinary cop or detective. Whoever he worked for her knew exactly who Aaron was, he knew who he had been and the things he had done and the only people that knew that were deep in the government.

"I can't say the same about you. There's something familiar about you but I can't put my finger on why."

Aaron took the outstretched hand, the other man's hand was warm and his handshake was firm. At least that was a good sign but it could simply have all been a part of whatever elaborate cover had been created. The men Aaron knew who were in charge of his division of Special Ops had been trained liars, there was nothing about them that could ever be trusted.

"It must be all of your years away from us, you've lost your edge."

McKinley smiled but it was the smile of a shark and not a man Aaron ever wanted to end up on the wrong side of. Aaron didn't answer him, choosing instead to bite back whatever smart retort was hovering on the tip of his tongue.

When he remained silent, McKinley's smile widened further.

"It seems you've gotten smarter with age. I'd read that being a smart ass was your forte."

"I've learned that keeping my mouth shut gets me into less trouble and I learn more. People tend to ramble around silent men."

McKinley chuckled to himself as he moved around the room, his gaze raking over everything in sight. Aaron knew he was cataloguing everything in his mind, it was something he would have done himself, it was important to be familiar with ones surroundings.

"Why are you here?"

Aaron said, keeping his voice as even and mild mannered as he could. It was the last thing he wanted to do, and it was the last thing he felt. Mild mannered wasn't a mood he would have ever associated with himself but given the circumstances it was something he could try.

"I thought you and I might discuss that in private."

McKinley seemed to be particularly taken with the books that lined the walls behind Aaron's desk but it was simply a pretence and Aaron knew it.

"This is as private as it gets." Aaron gestured to the study.

McKinley turned and eyed Bennet and David. He didn't even bother with Toby and Aaron knew that he had simply dismissed the young detective as not worthy of attention.

"I thought we could have a conversation without the civilians."

Bennet coughed and spluttered and Aaron turned in time to see purple colour flush up over his face. He trembled with rage and Aaron couldn't blame him.

Bennet wasn't perfect and Aaron knew how terrified he was of Hank but he'd been involved from the beginning. He hadn't hidden from what was happening and he hadn't ever tried to hide or conceal what Hank was up to. The press were more than aware of Hank and what he was capable of. Of course they didn't have the ins and outs of his background but if Bennet had that information then Aaron knew he would have shared it with them to.

"Civilians? I think you have me confused with someone else."

Bennet's voice was barely recognisable and Aaron suppressed a smile.

McKinley smiled and it was the smile of a consummate liar, the smile of a politician.

"I'm sorry if your took offence, Detective Bennet, I meant civilian only because you're not military."

"Neither am I."

Aaron piped up a small smile of satisfaction crossing his lips as McKinley shot him an irritated look. The expression was quickly wiped away and his smile returned.

"Ex-military then, if we're going to be like that."

There was irritation in his voice that belied his smile and it only made Aaron happier.

"This is as private as it's going to get, I'm afraid. Anything you want to discuss with me can be discussed in front of the men that have faced Hank and lived to tell the tale, they deserve your respect."

"What I have to discuss with you is sensitive and not something that just anyone can hear. Bennet is a cop and I can accept him hearing what I have to say but your brother is nobody. He's not a cop or military, what I have to say does not concern him and I won't speak in freely in front of him."

Aaron turned and stared at David. He remained in his seat on the sofa, his polished shoes, resting nonchalantly on the edge of the small wooden coffee table in front of him. He'd replaced the glass on the table and had folded his arms. A smirk played around his lips but there was a hardness in his eyes that told Aaron he didn't trust McKinley.

Aaron couldn't blame his brother and he was inclined to trust him. David was good at reading others. He didn't have military training but he was no stranger to dangerous men and situations and he was the only person in the room that Aaron would have trusted implicitly to have his back if they were moving into hostile territory.

"They I don't think we have anything to discuss."

McKinley's mask of civility slipped completely, his anger at being questioned shone through his eyes and in the lines of his face. Aaron watched as he clenched his jaw in an attempt to control his temper but it was too late for that.

"I don't think you understand the gravity of the situation Mr Ashcroft. There are things we need to discuss, sensitive issues that need clarification and it can't be done with everyone else being privy to the them."

Aaron shook his head a laugh escaping him. He moved to the door and pulled it open.

"You come into my house and tell me who should and shouldn't be privy to sensitive information. You stand here in front of men who have stood by me in an attempt to bring Hank to heel and you have the cheek to tell me to turn my brother out.

"You are sorely mistaken, McKinley, if you think that will ever happen. I trust this man here," Aaron gestured to David who sat on the couch, "far more than I will ever trust you or the men you work for."

"You can't be serious. You asked for our help in this matter, Aaron, you wanted the information we have on Hank and now you're rejecting it because I insulted your sense of honour?"

"Aaron, I can step outside..."

David interjected in an attempt to quell the coming argument but it was too late.

McKinley was right, he had asked for their help. He had wanted them to point him in the right direction before any of this had blown up and Hank had taken Kirsty. They'd ignored his requests. He was ex-military and that didn't count for much when it came to active members like Hank.

"No."

Aaron's tone was forceful and his ribs ached with the pressure he was putting on them by standing for so long.

"I asked for help. I asked for you to intercede and ensure that a man that was still working for you wouldn't put a young woman's life in danger. You and your agency ignored my request. You deemed it unimportant, hysterical and slanderous I believe you called it. And now when everything has gone to hell you expect me to cooperate with you."

Aaron shook his head and leaned against the door in an attempt to give his body a slight reprieve but his breathing was growing more laboured with each deep breath he took. Each breath was getting shallower and shallower as the pain built.

"You're the ones who screwed up, you're the ones who need to cooperate with me. So you can go back and tell the guys in charge that I'm not interested in whatever little game they want to play. This has gone too far and regardless of your orders I will find Hank and put a stop to him."

McKinley practically vibrated with rage as he strode from the room and headed straight for the front door. He ripped it open and slammed it behind him. The sound of car tyres squealing and gravel spraying into the air followed his departure and the sudden silence in the study.

Aaron didn't say anything as he moved to the tall wing back chair he had vacated when Bennet arrived and he dropped down into it. Sweat trickled down his spine as he reached for the bottle of scotch but David was there before him. Aaron watched his brother pour a tall glass and he accepted it gratefully, swallowing down the liquid before closing his eyes in an attempt to slow his fraught breathing.

"What the hell was all that about?"

Bennet's voice cut through the fog of pain that filled Aaron's mind. He opened his eyes in time to watch Bennet drop down onto a seat across from him. Toby stood, Aaron knew how awkward he felt by the way he struggled to figure out what he should do with himself.

"You tell me, you brought him here."

Aaron answered, swallowing back the pain that threatened to flare up within him once more.

"He turned up at the station, I didn't have a choice but to bring him here when I received a phone call from the Chief telling me to bring him to you."

Aaron nodded, he understood what it felt like to have your hands tied by circumstances and those with more power than you.

"There was a time when I worked with Hank as part of Special Ops, I presume that McKinley is an agent from one of their divisions sent over to try and cover up the mess that Hank and we're creating."

Bennet visibly bristled at Aaron's words and he was forced to raise his hand to cut off the oncoming tirade.

"I don't mean we're making a mess of tracking Hank down, just that we're doing it so publicly."

"And what? They'd prefer if we told no one and let him do whatever in hell he wanted to do? Hurt whoever he wants to hurt because they don't like having a spotlight shone on them and their operations."

Bennet's voice was filled with bitterness and Aaron was instantly curious. Only someone who'd had first hand experience with people like McKinley and the people he worked for would sound so bitter.

"This isn't your first hay ride is it?"

Aaron smiled but it was an act so he could watch Bennet closely.

The other man sighed and shook his head before reaching out for the bottle.

"Sir, is that wise?"

Toby immediately interjected. He rocked nervously back and forth on the balls of his feet as he watched Bennet pick up the bottle of scotch and lift it to his nose.

"I don't need someone to fret over me like a mother hen, Toby. I have no intention of drinking, I just want the smell…"

Aaron watched as he closed his eyes and inhaled deeply.

"I can get you a spare glass if you want?"

David said, pushing to his feet.

Bennet shook his head and replaced the bottle on the table.

"No thanks... I'm on the job."

"How long have you been sober?"

Aaron asked, sitting up in his seat. Pain roared through his body again and at that moment he would have given anything for some of the magic painkillers they'd had in the hospital.

"Two years now and it's not a place I want to go back to. But every so often I feel myself wanting to slip, like now, taking a big whiff is enough for now... I just have no idea how long it will stay enough."

"The case is a tough one, I suppose you find yourself needing the crutch of smelling it more and more often..."

Bennet dropped his gaze to the floor and Aaron knew he was right. The last thing he wanted to do was make the other man feel ashamed. What he had achieved was amazing, there were so many others out there not strong enough to overcome an addiction that was so strong.

"We'll get him, Bennet, we'll stop him and you'll realise just how strong you were."

"I just don't know how much longer I can keep it up. We got the results back on the heart in the box. They matched it to the Jane Doe we found. As far as we know Kirsty is still alive and he's still torturing her."

"And this other girl, do we know how long he had her?"

Bennet shook his head but the look in his eyes was haunted.

"No, we can't find her in the system and because we don't have the I.D it makes it that much harder to pinpoint how long he likes to cycle with them."

"What about her injuries? If he's keeping them for long periods of time then surely there is evidence of the abuse over a long period of time, remodelling of the bone after breaks."

Bennet nodded, "The postmortem results aren't entirely conclusive. Her body was badly decomposed but they seem to think that there was extensive damage and remodelling. I haven't heard if they've pinpointed a time frame yet but once they do I'll pass the information on."

Aaron smiled grimly. It was the best he could hope for, at least if he knew what the other girl suffered then he would have a clearer picture of what he had left Kirsty open to. At least if he had a time frame then he would know how much time she had before he grew bored of her.

The room fell silent and Aaron realised that the others were dwelling on the thought of sustained abuse over a long period of time. It was a gruesome thought and not something he would have wished on his worst enemy.

Not even Jude?

The small voice in the back of his mind piped up instantly making him uncomfortable. Jude was the one exception to the entire situation. Aaron didn't consider him to be an enemy, not anymore, he was far worse than that.

Jude was someone who had tried to steal the most precious people in his life from him and that wasn't something Aaron could ever forgive. The thought of leaving Hank alone with Jude however, filled him with dread. Monsters had a terrible habit of finding common ground and Aaron had no doubt that both men would join forces if they thought it would help in their survival.

A thought hit him then and he sat bolt upright in the chair. It couldn't possibly be true though, it seemed utterly impossible and it was something he hadn't even contemplated before now.

What if Hank and Jude already knew of each other? What if they were already plotting together?

"I know that look, Aaron."

David said, sitting back on the sofa.

"It's probably nothing."

Bennet shook his head and sat forward on the chair he had taken.

"I'll share everything I have, Ashcroft, as long as you do the same. We don't know what's important, the slightest thing could help."

Aaron contemplated making something up, if he was right then the last thing he really wanted to do was tip his hand. But if he was right then wasn't it in everyone's best interests if they knew the truth.

Aaron let the sight of the bruises down Bennet's face and the cast on his arm slowly sink in. Bennet wanted Hank as much as he did.

"We haven't looked into the fact that Jude could be playing a role in all of this."

Bennet's expression became confused and Aaron knew that he really hadn't put both men together as a possibility.

"Why would they work together? Aren't their motives at odds with one another?"

Aaron shook his head and pushed up onto his feet. He made his way to the window and stared out into the cold watery midday sun.

"I don't think so. They both blame me for ruining their lives, spoiling their fun. The only time they might come to blows is if Hank ever laid a hand on Heather…"

Aaron's stomach churned uncomfortably at the thought. He wouldn't ever let Hank get his hands on Heather, not if he could help it.

"Do you think she's at risk?"

Bennet's voice was low, almost guarded and it made Aaron smile. The detective was clever and he was quickly learning. Aaron knew from the low tone of his voice that he was hoping to slip the question in.

Aaron turned back to the other men gathered in the room and nodded.

"She's at risk as soon as Hank grows bored of Kirsty. Until we have an approximate time line for how long he likes to keep his victims we won't know how much time we have."

Bennet stood and swayed almost unsteadily on his feet for a moment. He regained his composure and sighed.

"I'll get back onto the forensics team, ask them to concentrate on getting us a timeline."

Bennet turned and started for the door but then seemed to change his mind. He paused and turned back to Aaron.

"What do you think he plans on doing with the kid?"

"Karl?"

Aaron said, surprised that Bennet was bringing him up. Bennet nodded, the look on his face telling Aaron that he was expecting to hear the worst.

"Once he's served his purpose Hank will kill him. He won't leave him around as a loose end that might trip him up."

"I thought you might say that. Was there ever a time when he wasn't such a cold hearted bastard?"

The question caught Aaron off guard and for a moment he wasn't sure how he was supposed to answer the question. There was a time when he would have trusted Hank with his life but he had no way of knowing if that was simply naive loyalty. Now he knew Hank better and a leopard didn't change its spots. If he was to believe that then it meant there was never a time when Hank could have been trusted. Each time he'd gone into a situation with Hank at his back, Aaron realised it had to be sheer luck that he'd survived.

"Once, I would have said he was one of the most trust worthy men I'd ever met. Even now I'd still say he could be trusted."

Bennet's expression went from one of cold anger to shock.

"You can't honestly mean that?"

Aaron nodded. "I do mean it. Hank is extremely trust worthy, I can trust that he will do whatever benefits him. I can trust him to always choose the cruelest methods of hurting others. And I know I can trust him to pick a date and time for when we will meet face to face and only one of us will walk away."

Aaron kept his voice devoid of any emotion. It was easier to talk about it if he shut his thoughts off. There would be no room for emotion if he did face Hank. Hank wouldn't be limited by emotions and he would be counting on the fact that Aaron couldn't stand idly by while people were hurt.

Of course he was right and Aaron wouldn't stand by and let Hank destroy lives, not if he could stop him anyway. But Hank would try and play on his emotions and that was something Aaron couldn't allow.

"You talk about it as though in the end it will just be the two of you."

Bennet's words made Aaron smile, he was smart and he was learning but there was so much that he hadn't yet grasped.

"In the end it will just come down to the two of us. I made the mistake of not putting a stop to Hank a long time ago and this is a mistake only I can fix. I'm not about to let anyone else take the fall for me, not if I can help it."

"And what about me in all of this, Aaron? What about your daughter?"

The door to the office swung open and Heather stood framed in the door. Her eyes snapped with anger and Aaron could practically feel the rage and fear that rolled off her skin. She was the last person he'd wanted to hear his declaration.

"Heather, I…"

He was at a loss for words. She stood and watched him, and Aaron felt his heart swell with pride. She was so strong, so fierce. He knew she would do anything to protect the people she loved, there was no doubt about that. He'd watched her time and again sacrifice herself in order to protect her loved ones and Aaron knew if given the chance to protect him that she would take it.

That knowledge left him with the bitter taste of fear in his mouth.

A moment passed between them and uncertainty flickered in Heather's eyes. He watched it flash there for a moment and then she turned from him and disappeared out into the hall.

Chapter Twelve

I STALKED OUT INTO THE hall and headed straight for the stairs.

Who the hell did he think he was? He couldn't make decisions like that, not a decision that could rip us all apart. It was stupid and selfish, arrogant even. And yet there he was in the study making sweeping declarations about how he would be the one to face Hank. How he would be the only one to face him.

There was no thought for me, for what we shared and Arianna couldn't have been further from his mind. What good would it do if Hank killed him? I refused to raise Arianna on my own because her father was too stubborn to ask for, or accept help.

"Heather, wait!"

Aaron's voice followed me as I reached the top of the stairs but I didn't stop. Instead I moved down the hall in the direction of the our bedroom. I didn't want to hear his excuses, his reasons for what he had said. As far as I was concerned it was all perfectly clear and I didn't need to hear anymore.

The creaking of the stairs told me he was gaining on me and I picked up my pace as I approached the bedroom door.

Swinging into the bedroom, I fumbled to shut the door but with one easy thrust Aaron pushed the door open. There was a fine sheen of sweat on his face and I could see the pain in his eyes. Clearly hurrying after me had cost him.

He stood in the doorway, his breathing a little heavier than normal.

I wanted to feel bad, guilty that I had caused him pain but if I was honest with myself I just couldn't bring myself to feel it. I'd caused him pain but he'd done the same to me.

"Heather, you weren't supposed to hear that."

"I realise that. Were you going to tell me what your plans were? Did you even care how I might have felt about it all?"

"You know I have to do this, I can't let him go on hurting others... He's my problem, my responsibility."

I shook my head and laughed, a short bitter sound.

"Your responsibility? So you turned him into the monster he is? You forced him to hurt people? You made him take Kirsty, you made him torture her?"

My voice became choked with emotion and I struggled to fight it back. He wasn't making any sense. How could he feel responsible for someone as messed up as Hank?

"No, it's not like that... You don't understand, Heather, I can't expect you to understand why I have to do this, I just need you to let me get on with it."

I took one trembling step forward, the sound of my hand connecting with his face filled the room with a crack. Shock washed over me as I realised what I had done.

"Don't you dare tell me I need to accept your misguided suicide mission. You want to leave me, leave Arianna and I'm supposed to just accept it."

Aaron shook his head, his hand sliding across his jaw, massaging the spot where I had slapped him. I could see the beginning of my hand print blossoming in red across his cheek.

"Heather, it's not like that, I don't expect you to accept just anything but you know I have to do this."

"And can you promise me that you won't get hurt or worse?"

He shook his head and dropped his face into his hands.

"You know I can't promise you that."

"Then you can't ask me to be alright with this. If anything happened to you, Aaron, what would I do? What would I do without you, what would Arianna do?"

"I think you're overreacting. I thought you trusted me, that you knew I would always do what was right. I thought you trusted me to always come back to you..."

His words overwhelmed me and tears started down my face. Turning from him I buried my face in my hands and sobbed.

It wasn't fair, none of it was fair. All I'd ever wanted was right here, within my grasp and now I was supposed to simply accept that I might have to give it up because it was the right thing to do? I wouldn't do it without a fight.

Aaron's arms closed around me, his body pressing to mine as he rocked my body in against his.

"I won't do it. I'm not going to let you destroy us."

"Heather, I have no intention of destroying us."

"Why do you always have to be so stubborn? You have people who want to help you, you're not alone in any of this and you're behaving as though you're the only one on the planet who can stop Hank. Surely you have to know that working with others is better? That you stand a better chance of succeeding if you let them help you?"

I could feel his head shake against my shoulder and I groaned with frustration.

"Heather, I love you, I love you more than I've ever loved anyone in my life and there won't ever be a moment when I don't love you. But you need to know that I always fix my own mistakes. Too many have already suffered because I couldn't do what needed to be done a long time ago."

"What do you mean?"

He sighed and turned me in his grip. My hands automatically wrapped around his waist, drawing our bodies even closer together. Even though we were arguing, even though I was angrier than I'd ever been in my life with him, I still wanted to be near him. I didn't want any distance between us.

"I've known Hank wasn't right for a long time. And for too long I ignored it, I let him go and live his life and I didn't interfere."

My mouth dropped open and I felt the blood in my veins turn to ice.

"You knew about the things he did and..."

Aaron cut me off before I could complete my sentence with a shake of his head.

"No I never knew about his torturing and killing of people. Well I never had proof of it. The last mission we did together I think I had my suspicions, if my dreams are anything to go by then I had more than suspicions but something happened and I don't have all the pieces of that final night anymore."

"How can you not have all the pieces of that night?"

I asked, my voice incredulous as I stared up at him. This was the man I loved, the father of my child and now I was starting to wonder if I knew him at all.

Aaron pulled away from me and strode across the room. His shoulders were tense and I knew he was angry but I had no clue why.

"This is why I never wanted you to know about my past with Hank. How can I explain something to you that I don't even fully understand myself? What if he's right and I'm just as much the monster as he is?"

I followed him across the room until I could face him.

"You're nothing like him, you could never be anything like him."

"But how do you know? I know something terrible happened and yet I kept silent about it all this time. I brought him into our lives and I didn't think that I might be putting you at risk."

Realisation hit me then. I remembered the guilty look on his face from the night when Hank had sent the package. I remembered the way he had apologised over and over as though he was the one at fault. He felt responsible, as though he could control what Hank did.

"Aaron, you can't blame yourself for this, it isn't your fault, none of this is your fault. You need to believe me."

He shook his head and tried to turn from me but I held him. My hands slid up to his face and I gripped him tightly refusing to let him turn from me. He had to know that he wasn't a monster, that he wasn't like Hank. People made mistakes, we were only human and god only knew but I had made my fair share of bad choices and mistakes myself but this wasn't something he could hold against himself.

"You're nothing like him, do you hear me?"

"You don't know that for certain."

"Yes, Aaron, yes I do know that. I know you. You're the man I love, the father of my child. You have a good heart, a pure heart. I know you'd never hurt anyone not intentionally. I know the guilt you carry and I know how wrong it is…"

"Heather, you can't be certain of that, no one can. Unless I remember…"

I cut him off with a kiss, my lips finding his in a desperate and all consuming kiss. I clung to him, crushing my body to his as I poured everything into the kiss. I needed him to feel what I felt, needed him to feel the truth in my embrace.

His tongue slid along my lips and I opened to him, my lips parting granting him access to my mouth. We came together hard and violent, Aaron's hands sliding down over my back to my ass. He dug his fingers in hard against my flesh making me cry out softly against his mouth.

He pushed his body against mine, walking me backwards until the back of my legs hit the edge of the bed.

I fumbled with the front of his shirt, struggling to open it and pull it off over his shoulders. Our mouths barely parted as we continued to kiss, his hands stripped me from my clothes. The moment his fingers found my exposed nipples I gasped, he pinched and teased them to life drawing small gasps of pleasure from my lips.

He pushed the jeans I wore down over my hips and I stepped out of them, quickly discarding them to one side as Aaron pushed me down beneath him on the bed.

My fingers danced across the edge of the white bandages that covered his chest and I chewed my lip. I'd come so close to losing him, so close to my entire life crumbling around me.

"What are you thinking?"

Aaron's mouth moved down over my neck as he crawled up between my legs. I groaned as he bit down on my shoulder drawing a whimper of desire from me.

"I nearly lost you, Aaron, I nearly lost all of this…"

My voice trailed off as it became choked with emotion. How could I explain to him how much he meant to me, that the thought of almost losing him was enough to stop my heart in my chest.

"But you didn't, I'm here with you, I'll always be right here with you."

His fingers found the soaking wet entrance to my body and I bucked beneath his touch. My eyes rolled back in my head, tears soaking into my eye lashes as I struggled to keep breathing.

Aaron's hand pressed against me, his fingers pushing deeper into my body, opening me up to him. His tongue laved over my nipple and I cried out, the pleasure of his caress almost too much to bear.

I dug my nails into his shoulders as he continued to work at my body, the rising ebb and flow of pleasure swelling within me until it couldn't be ignored anymore.

As though he knew I was close he slipped his fingers out of me, positioning his body between my legs. The feel of his hard thickness pressing against the opening to my sex had me writhing beneath him.

LOVING THE BILLIONAIRE EVER AFTER

Opening my eyes I stared up at him. His dark eyes seemed darker and I could see the pain it caused him to prop his body above mine. It filled his eyes with an intensity I didn't think was possible and as he thrust up into me the full weight of his body crushed down over mine.

I gasped for air, struggling to breathe against the pressure of having him push up and against my body. Aaron's mouth found mine once more, his kiss stealing the little amount of air I had in my lungs.

Each thrust was hard won, each one sending him deeper inside me, opening me a little more to his thick hard flesh. He groaned against my lips and as I opened my eyes again I realised that he was staring down into my face.

The intensity of our love making was enough to push me into an explosively pleasurable orgasm. It ripped through me and I cried out into his kiss.

My body bucked and heaved as my eyes rolled back in my head, every inch of me awash in tingling sensation.

Aaron bit down on my lip, his own cry muffled as it mingled with mine. My body was acutely aware of every little move he made, and his final hard thrust had white light exploding behind my eye lids.

He pushed up inside me as though he was trying to ensure that the pleasure he spilled within me would stay inside me.

Warmth pulsed through my body and I clamped my legs around his waist in an attempt to hold him in place.

We clung to each other like two lovers cast adrift in a sea of pleasure. I never wanted the moment to end, never wanted to lose the feeling of him inside me.

Tears filled my eyes and spilled down over my cheeks. I kept my eyes closed even as Aaron lifted his body away from mine. I fought the urge to grab at him, to hold his body to mine.

Cold air swirled in around my body, cooling the sweat that coated my skin.

"Heather, what's the matter? Did I hurt you?"

His voice was very near my ear and filled with concern. The feel of his fingers as they brushed softly against my tear soaked cheeks only made me cry harder.

"Heather, what did I do?"

I shook my head unable to answer him. How could I explain it? Here I was lying in the bed beside him sobbing my heart out because I was a confused mix of happy and sad. It wasn't exactly something that could easily be explained away.

"I'm sorry I was clumsy, Heather, I didn't mean to hurt you."

The sound of his voice broke my heart and I had no idea why. I rolled towards him and wrapped my arms around his body.

"You didn't hurt me, I don't know how to explain it..."

Tentatively he wrapped his arms around my shoulders drawing my body in against him.

"It's everything, Aaron. It's Jude and now this with Hank…"

"Wait what about Jude?"

"They want me to testify, I have to attend a meeting tomorrow to discuss what will be expected of me."

Aaron's body stiffened and I stared up at him.

"What is it? What did I say?"

He shook his head but I could see from the look on his face that something had clearly bothered him.

"When did you get the letter? The attorney was supposed to ensure that you were kept out of all of that."

I shook my head and shrugged.

"It doesn't really matter, it was stupid to think that I might be able to get out of facing him. And anyway, I wouldn't mind seeing his face when the judge throws the book at him."

Aaron nodded but it was obvious that there was something bothering him. He clearly didn't want to share it with me and the thought that he would keep secrets from me, especially about something so important bothered me.

"If you knew something you would tell me wouldn't you?"

"Of course I would."

I could hear the lie in his voice and it surprised me. Aaron had never been a liar and it seemed the situation with Hank had turned him into one.

His hand stroked up and down my back and as hard as I fought it sleep finally washed over me. There was no peace to be found in my dreams and at every turn I was besieged with images of Aaron hurt or dead at the hands of Hank.

The nightmares woke me suddenly, my body enveloped in a fine sheen of sweat. I lay in the dark, Aaron's side of the bed empty but I could hear his voice. Arianna's familiar gurgling was interrupted only by Aaron's whispered voice and I lay in the dark listening to the two most important people in my life.

It was a moment that should have filled me with happiness and yet I couldn't shake the images from the nightmare. I couldn't let Aaron face Hank alone. I knew he was strong, that he was more than capable but there was something about Hank that terrified me. He was utterly devoid of human feeling and the thought of him laying hands on Aaron was enough to reduce me to tears. I knew without doubt that if both men met it would end in tragedy and I couldn't stand the idea of Aaron not coming home to me.

There had to be something I could do, some way to stop Hank and yet if I was honest I had no idea what it was. I didn't know him and I had no clue where he might be, even if I did what was I going to do that would stop him?

When Jude had been hunting me I'd felt afraid, scared for those I loved but I'd never once felt as helpless as I did now. There had to be something I could do... I just had no clue what it was. My only hope was that it would come to me.

Chapter Thirteen

*S*ITTING IN THE PRISON VISITING room, Aaron let his mind wander back to the time he had spent holding Arianna in his arms as Heather had slept. If he could have remained frozen that moment forever he would have but it was impossible.

Heather had still been sleeping when he'd left at first light. The last thing he wanted was for her to find out about what he was up to.

The sound of doors slamming shut drew Aaron's attention and he glanced up as the guards brought Jude down the long corridor. The sound of the cuffs and chains filled Aaron with pleasure, he could only hope that this was a state that Jude would always find himself in.

Pushing open the secure door the guards moved Jude inside and secured him on the opposite side of the table to where Aaron sat.

A shadow of a smile hovered around Jude's lips and Aaron couldn't help but wonder what exactly a man like Jude could have to smile about. Being in prison couldn't exactly be something that he was enjoying, of that Aaron was certain.

"I didn't expect to see you here."

Jude said, the smile on his face widening as he settled himself into the hard metal chair that was bolted to the floor.

"Don't lie, Jude, you know exactly why I'm here."

Aaron kept his voice as even as he could, the urge to lunge across the table and smash Jude's face against the table top was almost overwhelming. But it wouldn't solve anything and it wouldn't help him get to Hank.

"I'm almost positive I have no clue why you're visiting me. Unless of course you've grown bored of Heather and you want to hand her back to me?"

Jude's tone was filled with hope and Aaron clenched his fists hard enough to turn his knuckles white. He was utterly insufferable and Aaron wanted nothing more than to be as far from him as he could.

"Where is he, Jude?"

There was a flicker of recognition in Jude's eyes but it was gone in an instant. Instead, Jude leaned back in the chair his expression unreadable.

"Where is who?"

"Hank, I know he came to see you, I know you two have spoken."

"And why should I share anything with you? You destroyed my life, put me in the hospital, sent the cops poking into my affairs."

Aaron sighed, he wasn't going to get anything from Jude unless there was something he could offer him. As far as Aaron was concerned there was nothing he could offer, well nothing he wanted to offer anyway.

"He's set his sights on Heather."

It was the only thing Aaron could think to say. It was a risk but Aaron was counting on the fact that once Jude latched onto a girl he didn't let go until he was completely satisfied.

Jude smiled but his expression wasn't as confident or as smug as it had been.

"He has no interest in interfering with my work."

Aaron laughed, the sound echoing around the small empty room.

"Your work? Jude, you're never getting out of here. Once your case comes up they'll throw the book at you and you'll be nothing but a footnote on Heather's life. Hank isn't confined the way you are. I can see from the look on your face that you're worried. You know what he's capable of, you know what he'll do if he's allowed to carry on unchecked."

Jude shook his head a fine tremble beginning to work its way through his body.

"We made a deal, he agreed that Heather was mine, no matter what, it's you he wants."

"And what would you do if you wanted to hurt me, Jude? What's the key to completely destroying my life?"

Jude fell silent, a look of anger and distrust crossing his face but he remained stubbornly silent.

"Jude, tell me so I can stop him from hurting Heather."

"He won't hurt her, he knows the consequences aren't worth it."

Aaron fell silent, an uncomfortable feeling filling him.

"What do you mean? You seem to be very sure that he hasn't already tried to hurt her?"

Jude smiled but he didn't say anything.

A knock on the window drew Aaron's attention and he turned to see one of the guards gesturing for him to come to the door.

Aaron didn't want to leave, Jude knew something, something he wasn't sharing but Aaron knew it was something worth having. There had to be a way to get the truth out of him.

"I don't think they're going to stop until you see what they want."

Aaron growled with frustration and stood, moving to the door. He paused with his hand on the handle.

"If anything happens to her I will kill you."

"Even your reach doesn't extend this far, Ashcroft. In here I'm the safest I've ever been."

Aaron didn't turn to look at him, he didn't need to he could already imagine the arrogant look on Jude's face.

"That's where you're wrong, Jude. If Hank hurts her, if he…"

Aaron broke off, unable to bring himself to finishing the sentence. He sucked in a deep breath before he continued.

"If anything happens to her, there is nowhere on this earth that you'll be safe from me. I will hunt you down like the animal you are and I will put a bullet between your eyes and I don't care what it takes… Just keep that in mind."

Aaron pushed open the door and stepped out into the room beyond. The guard that had been knocking on the window looked at him with a strange sideways glance. It was the look he usually got when people underestimated him and then suddenly realised how dangerous he could potentially be. It was a look that told him the guard was suddenly reevaluating him and how to handle him.

Aaron smiled, a charming disarming look. It was a look that told the guard he meant no harm and that he would get no trouble from him.

Aaron hadn't wanted any witnesses to his threat to Jude but at the end of the day he didn't care. If anything happened to Heather then there wouldn't be anything left to live for or care about. Witnesses to idle threats didn't particularly matter, if the worst ever happened then no one would stop him from carrying it out.

"Is there something wrong?"

Aaron dropped his voice, keeping it light and friendly. The guard dropped his gaze but Aaron caught him casting sideways glances in his direction. He flipped open a file on the desk in front of him.

"You've got a phone call from an Agent McKinley."

Aaron opened his mouth to dismiss it but the guard stopped him.

"McKinley, said you wouldn't want to take the phone call so he said to tell you there's new information and you're going to want it."

If there was new information then why hadn't Bennet told him about it? Surely the leading Detective on the case would know whatever McKinley was going to tell him, so why hadn't Bennet shared it? He'd said he would share whatever information he had, that they would work together.

There was a bad feeling in the pit of Aaron's stomach, one that he couldn't shake no matter how hard he tried.

He nodded and followed the guard from the room and down the corridor to the telephone. He scooped it up and pressed the phone to his ear.

"How did you track me down here, McKinley."

Aaron struggled not to sound irritated on the phone and failed.

Laughter froze the blood in his veins, it wasn't McKinley's voice on the other end of the line.

"I see you're not a fan of Agent McKinley either, that's good to know."

Hank sounded happy and relaxed and the sound of his voice grated on the inside of Aaron's head.

"How did you know I'd be here?"

"How did I know?" There was more laughter and Aaron fought to bring his breathing back to a more normal rate. "I know everything you do, Aaron. I know where you go, I know how close you are. Everything you know I've fed to you because I wanted you to have it."

"So why pretend to be McKinley to get me on the phone?"

There was silence for a moment as though Hank hadn't honestly thought of an appropriate response to a question like that.

"I wanted to know what you really thought of him. I wanted to know if he was one of your allies. He seems to think you're both on the same side."

"I don't understand, Hank, how could McKinley think that we were allies... How do you know what he's thinking?"

The sound of movement on the other end of the line had Aaron straining to listen harder. It sounded as though Hank was walking, the sound of footsteps followed by the muffled sounds of something, crying for help. Aaron couldn't honestly tell, all he knew for certain was that the sound filled him with a cold fear.

"Is that, Kirsty?"

Aaron asked, his stomach flipping uncomfortably.

"Guess again."

Aaron could hear the smile in Hank's voice.

"If you kill me you're going to bring the full wrath of the government down on your head, Hank, you don't want to do this."

McKinley sounded honestly frightened and Aaron had to wonder what Hank had done to him to make him sound like that.

"Hank, what the hell are you doing? McKinley is innocent in all of this, you have to let him go. This is between you and me, no one else needs to be involved."

"You're right about one thing, Aaron, this is between you and me and McKinley had to ruin that... He can't be sniffing around."

Aaron heard the sound of the safety being clicked off a gun. He could practically see the scene playing out in his mind like he was there watching it all.

"Hank, you can't do this."

Aaron's tone went up as the sound of McKinley's muffled cries grew more and more frantic.

"He wants to ruin us both, Aaron. If I don't get rid of him he'll find a way to pin all of this on you... It was his plan all along, he knows everything..."

The sound of the gun going off was enough to rock Aaron on his feet. The silence that followed was filled by the sound of his heart beat hammering in his ears.

"I did this for you, Aaron, this is between us."

Hank's voice filtered slowly through into Aaron's shocked mind. He wasn't even sure why he was shocked, it made perfect sense that Hank would do something so heinous. McKinley wouldn't be the first person he had killed.

"You killed him... He's dead?"

"I'll leave his body somewhere it can be easily found. I thought you'd have understood why I had to do this."

A hint of petulance had crept into Hank's voice and that was all it took to send Aaron over the edge. What was the point of being calm? What was the point of trying to talk to Hank as though he was someone who could be reasoned with? He was a lunatic, a mad man who had no issues with putting a bullet in anyone who got in his way.

"You're mad, off your head if you thought I would understand that, Hank? You murdered someone and you had me listen while you did it. I'll never be alright with that, no one in their right mind would ever be alright with that."

Aaron's outburst was followed by silence and then the line went dead. He replaced the phone handset on its cradle and stared down at it.

"What happened?"

Aaron jumped as he realised the guard that had called him the meeting with Jude was still standing in the room with him. He turned and stared at the young man standing near the door.

"What did you hear?"

"You started to shout so I came in to see what the fuss was about."

Aaron sighed and started for the door. The guard tried to block his path, his hand pressing into Aaron's chest as he attempted to force him back.

"I said what happened, it sounded serious."

"It was serious. Now if you want your hand to stay attached to your arm then I would advise you remove it from me immediately."

"Does it have anything to do with the prisoner Jude Fossen?"

Aaron shook his head in irritation and stared at the man standing in front of him.

"What the hell has that got to do with anything? That phone call was none of your business, now get the hell out of my way."

Aaron started to push past the guard, his hand knocking the guards away from his chest. The guard moved in against him, both hands coming up to grab the front of Aaron's jacket. But Aaron saw him coming and he was more than ready for him. Without even having to think about what he was doing, he blocked the grab the guard made, driving him back against the wall of the small phone room. He pinned him there, his hands pressed up under the other man's throat.

Within seconds the room was filled with other guards, their hands closing around his arms as they hauled him away. Aaron was left with no choice but to surrender and let them subdue him.

"What were you thinking, Mr Ashcroft?"

The prison warden sat on his side of the desk, his fingers steepled in front of him as Aaron watched him. Aaron's ribs ached as though someone had kicked him repeatedly but he knew it wasn't the after effects of a booted foot that he was feeling. All it took was a well placed punch or two from some of the more overly zealous guards to send his already injured ribs into overdrive.

"I told you I wasn't thinking, I reacted. I have to talk to Detective Bennet, there's some very sensitive information pertaining to an ongoing case that I need to share with him. The longer you detain me here, the more I fear the situation will worsen."

"Son, one of my men is saying that you threatened the life of one of my inmates… Now I'm not stupid, I realise that none of the prisoners are here because they're fine upstanding gentlemen. And I'm no stranger to what Jude Fossen has been charged with but that doesn't mean you can simply waltz into my prison and do whatever in hell you like."

Warden Silas Granger sat back against the plush leather backed chair he was perched in. Aaron contemplated what would happen if he reached across the desk and shook the man. Too much time had passed, Hank had probably already had time to dump the body and moved on. Sitting here with the warden was like being stuck in a constant loop of stupidity and the more Aaron tried to tell him that there was more important things at stake than Jude's safety, the more Granger dug his heels in.

"I know, and I said I was sorry. It was an idle threat and one I would never follow through on. Now can you please contact Detective Bennet so I can speak to him."

"You rich men all behave the same, you think your money makes you immune, you think it makes you special. It doesn't, in the end we're all equal when they put us in the ground."

There was a quiet knock on the door and Aaron sat back on his hard plastic chair with a frustrated sigh. The longer he was kept here, the more time Hank had to plan his next move.

Aaron had made a mistake, enraging Hank had been stupid and now Aaron could only hope that someone he cared about wouldn't pay the price for his stupidity.

The door swung inwards and the young receptionist that Aaron had seen outside stepped into the room. She moved towards the desk, her timidity making Aaron idly curious. A prison seemed like the last place a person as unsure as her would work and yet here she was. She paused alongside Granger and whispered into his ear.

Aaron watched as his shoulders stiffened and he stood fast enough to drive his chair back against the grey wall behind him.

"They have no business barging in here, this is my prison."

Granger's voice was filled with anger as he started to move around his desk. He didn't make it very far before the door flopped open again with a bang.

"We did ask nicely, Warden, if you're not willing to hand Mr Ashcroft over to us then we'll be forced to take him."

Aaron spun on his chair, his interest suddenly piqued. The men standing in the door all wore the same plain black suits as McKinley had. Their hair all had the same uniform cut and the expression's they wore were the same ones Aaron had witnessed on the faces of his superiors whenever they were forced to stonewall someone.

Aaron had no idea how long McKinley had been missing for but the fact that they were here looking for him meant they knew something was wrong. Had Hank kept his word and left the body somewhere easy to find?

"You have no jurisdiction here."

Aaron smiled to himself and he was forced to admit that he admired Granger just a little. In all his years working for Special Ops, Aaron hadn't seen many men with the guts to stand up to those in charge.

"Mr Ashcroft is not a prisoner here, I think you'll find you're the one with no jurisdiction."

The man who had done all the talking seemed to be the one in charge and as he inclined his head slightly one of the other men stepped forward and dropped a folded piece of paper on the table.

Granger scooped it up and hastily ripped it open. Aaron watched his face with interest as it changed colour, going from a slight pink to a full on angry puce.

"Mr Ashcroft, if you'd like to follow us please."

The one in charge gestured for Aaron to follow him. There was a moment of indecision. Aaron didn't owe these people anything anymore, he'd already given them more than enough. But he couldn't shake the image in his mind of what Hank had done and the way he had done it. It seemed so cold and callous. The least Aaron could do at this point was share that information with them. McKinley was one of theirs after all and if they didn't already know about his death, then Aaron felt he owed it to them, to McKinley to help in the search for his body.

He stood and headed for the door, leaving Granger to silently fume while he screwed the sheet of paper up in his hand.

There was silence as Aaron followed the three men out of the warden's office and down the hall. He knew only too well that there would be complete silence until they reached the safety of somewhere quiet and secure. And once they did and Aaron shared what he knew with them, all hell would break loose.

Chapter Fourteen

RATHER THAN WAIT FOR DESIGNATED date I was supposed to meet with the attorney I headed over there the first chance I got. The fact that Aaron had left so early in the morning certainly made it easier to sneak away.

Arianna was to small to know where we were going and as I sat waiting in the attorney's waiting room she cooed softly as I rocked her in her stroller. Staring down into her tiny face she reminded me so much of Aaron. The thought of him out there hunting Hank down alone made my stomach churn painfully. I'd discovered the only way to really get any sort of relief was to try and force myself to not think about what Aaron might be up to.

It didn't change the fact that I knew deep down, but it was like masking the issue and it at least gave me some superficial relief.

"Mr Coffrey will see you now."

The secretary spoke, a sullen look on her face as she addressed me.

Standing I waled past her, pushing Arianna ahead of me into the large spacious office. The room itself was what I would have imagined the perfect man cave to be. Everything seemed to be made of highly polished dark wood. It gave everything the air of being terribly expensive.

"Mrs Ashcroft, so nice you could come in and see us. I must admit to being a little surprised to seeing you here at the moment. I don't believe our appointment was due for another week?"

"I didn't want it hanging over me. It's not something to look forward to."

Mr Coffrey nodded sympathetically and I fought the urge to ask him if he had ever been in the same position as me or was his smile simply a well practiced lie. Perhaps that was the reason we were paying him such a large fee.

"I understand that urge completely. May I call you, Heather?"

I nodded, there didn't seem to be a point in denying him.

"So what exactly was on your mind, Heather?"

"I want you to tell me what I have to do."

He nodded and stood, moving towards a large filing cabinet in the corner. It seemed a little odd and old fashioned to still have files on paper. Most businesses were ran online and the files were all electronic. My face must have betrayed me because when he turned towards me and caught me staring he smiled and shrugged.

"I like the feel of paper and it's what I'm most comfortable with. The secretary still keeps everything on the computer but for me, it'll always be paper."

He fished a file from the drawer he was searching through and moved back to the desk. He sat and flipped through it, his eyes scanning the sheets of paper in front of him faster than I could follow.

When he finally glanced back his smile had dimmed.

"This must be very difficult for you."

I shrugged, unsure how to answer him. Arianna chose that moment to start crying, her small pitiful sobs making her impossible to ignore. I stood and scooped her from the stroller and rocked her softly in my arms.

"They'll put you on the stand, you'll be expected to go into detail over what Jude did to you…"

I could feel the colour draining from my face. The last thing I wanted was to spend my time reliving the horrible things Jude had done to me. It didn't seem fair that I would be forced to go back over everything, in fact it felt more like a punishment on me for turning him in, in the first place.

"I know it's not a nice thought…"

"Not a nice thought? That's an understatement. The things Jude Fossen did to me aren't exactly the type of things I want to ever have to think about. I'm forced to live with painful reminders of what he put me through."

"The scars?"

I nodded my mouth suddenly dry as though I had swallowed a mouthful of cotton wool.

"I realise how difficult it is and believe me when I say if I could save you the pain of having to go through all of this again then I would. Unfortunately there's only one way to achieve the goal we all want here and that's by putting you and your sister on the stand."

I sighed and arianna settled in against me. I stared down into her face my heart rate slowly returning to a more normal rate as I watched her tiny chest rise and fall with each breath she took.

"I'll do whatever it takes as long as he gets put away for good. That man deserves to have the key thrown away."

Mr Coffrey paused and dropped his gaze back to the files in front of him.

"Even with your testimony and that of your sisters, there's still no guarantee that he will receive a guilty verdict. As much as I'd love to tell you that it's a sure thing I can't do that…"

"So what I have to go on the stand and relive some of the most horrendous moments I ever had to get through and he still might get away with it?"

He nodded instead of answering me, as though he was ashamed of the truth himself.

"So what's the point of it? Why should I do it if the outcome might be so…"

I faltered, unsure how I should even continue. How could I explain how I felt, how the thought of him getting out and walking around made me feel physically ill? I stared down at Arianna. How was I supposed to keep her safe? How could I protect her if there was no real justice in the world?

"I know it isn't what you wanted to hear, it never is and if I can change it I would. But the reality at the end of the day is that men like Jude because they're so powerful they have access to fantastic lawyers. Usually when they fight back in a case like this they're doing so against a victim that isn't mentally strong enough to get through it. In your case, you are strong enough…"

"I don't know if I am anymore. With everything that's going on at the moment I don't know if I can take this on as well… It all seems like too much and I need to focus on the people who are most important in my life right now. I need to focus on Aaron and keeping Arianna safe…"

The cell phone in my bag buzzed noisily drawing my attention. Leaning over I picked it up, doing my best to keep Arianna in place against my shoulder.

"I'm sorry…"

The number was instantly recognisable as the phone from the warehouse office.

"Hello?"

I pressed the phone to my ear turning slightly from the attorney as though by doing that I was giving myself more privacy, or at the very least the illusion of privacy.

"Heather?"

Giselle sounded a little breathless and more than a little frightened.

"Hi, Giselle, what's wrong?"

"Heather, can you come down to the warehouse, I've called the cops but you're the owner and…"

"Giselle, what happened?"

There was a pause on the other end of the line and I could practically see Giselle trying to gather her thoughts before speaking.

"One of the girls went to pick up some extra fabric bolts from the back of the warehouse and…"

More silence.

I wanted to shout at her to tell me what was going on, to simply spit it out but I couldn't bring myself to do it. For some reason I didn't want to hear whatever it was that Giselle was about to tell me. I didn't want her to say it aloud, saying it aloud made it real and once it was real it couldn't ever be taken back.

"There was a body, Heather… There's a body in the back of the warehouse…"

Her voice trailed off until it was little more than a squeak. I opened my mouth to say something but there were no words to leave my mouth. My brain refused to come up with something useful I could say to her. There were no words of comfort I could give.

The only thought that swirled in my head, 'is it Kirsty?'

It circled around and around until I was sure I would simply go mad.

"A body?"

My voice finally broke through the wall of silence my brain had created and the first words out of my mouth were simply a repetition of what Giselle had just said.

"Heather, I don't know what to do, everyone is freaking out down here…"

"Giselle, calm down. I'll come straight over."

"Heather, who would have done something like this?"

"I don't know, Giselle." It was a lie but I figured a lie was better right now than the truth. I knew exactly who would do something like this but telling her might create panic.

"Just keep everyone away from it and I'll be there as soon as I can."

I started to stand as I spoke. Giselle didn't say anything else to me, the line going dead as she hung up. I could imagine the fear she felt, my stomach had dropped into my shoes just thinking about Hank and what he had done.

"Is everything alright?"

Mr Coffrey stood, his eyes filled with concern and I knew he had heard the conversation.

"It's fine but I need to go…"

He nodded and moved around the table to help me. I didn't say anything to him as I placed Arianna back in the stroller and headed for the door.

The drive over to the warehouse took less time than I anticipated and I found myself with practically no time to prepare myself for what I was about to walk in on. Pulling up in front of the building the police cars and yellow tape stopped me from getting too close.

Stepping out of the car I lifted Arianna in her car seat from the car. I had no one to mind her and although I didn't want to expose her to the situation I was left with no choice.

"Ma'am, I'm afraid this is a closed scene you can't come in here."

"My name is Heather Ashcroft, I own the warehouse, I think you'll want to talk to me."

The officer standing on the other side of the yellow shook his head.

"I can't let you cross the line, Ms Ashcroft."

I caught sight of Detective Bennet and quickly gestured in his direction.

"Ask, Detective Bennet, he'll tell you who I am."

Bennet caught my eye and turned a look of surprise on his face. He headed in my direction, pausing only once he reached the yellow tape line.

"I didn't expect to see you here, Heather, I tried to contact Aaron but his phone keeps on going direct to voicemail…"

An uneasy feeling opened up in the pit of my stomach. It wasn't like Aaron to have his cell phone off, especially now with someone like Hank on the loose.

"Did he contact you?" Bennet watched me, his eyes filled with curiosity.

"No, I received a phone call from the girl who runs the warehouse for me, Giselle told me there was a body in the back of the fabric room…"

Bennet's expression didn't change and I couldn't help but wonder how long it had taken him to perfect the cold icy expression he now wore. Bennet moved forward and lifted the yellow tape. I couldn't help but hesitate, it didn't make any sense, a few minutes before and I had wanted to cross the line. Now that Bennet was here holding the tape in the air for me to cross beneath I was suddenly hesitating. I couldn't explain why I felt nervous but I did. Part of me didn't trust Bennet, there was something about him that worried me. It was an irrational fear but one I had none the less.

I stepped forward and ducked beneath the tape. Bennet dropped it back into place and strode back toward the steps. Without knowing what else I should do, I followed him. I moved slower, my pace practically sluggish as I carried Arianna carefully through the crowds of workers and police officers gathered outside.

Bennet paused at the bottom of the steps, he waited for me to catch up to him before he started up them.

"Where are we going?"

I called after him but he didn't answer me, instead he carried on until he reached the door at the top of the steps and pulled it open. He stood without looking at me and held the door open. Once I reached the top step, I swapped my grip on Arianna's car seat to my other arm and paused.

"Detective, where are we going? You have me following you for a reason, what is it?"

My stomach was rapidly sinking into my shoes and I had a feeling that whatever Bennet had in mind was going to be something I would like.

"I'd prefer if you'd follow me and I'll answer all your questions once I show you what I need to."

"Is it, Kirsty?"

My heart shuddered to a halt as soon as I said her name aloud. I knew what it was like to be terrorised, I knew what it was like to be tortured and I knew how hard it was to pick the pieces of yourself back up. The thought that Hank had killed her, that she'd never had a chance to fight back made me want to cry.

"It's not Kirsty…"

Three simple words and I had the sudden urge to drop onto the top step and weep. I remained standing, struggling to keep my expression neutral. When Bennet didn't say anything else I moved past him and into the warehouse.

I heard Giselle before I saw her. Her voice was high and thready with panic and fear. As soon as I rounded the corner and stepped into the main floor of the warehouse I spotted her. Two officers stood in front of her, one with a notebook open in front of him and I could tell from the hand gestures she was making that she didn't feel as though she was being listened to.

"Heather!"

The relief in her voice as she called out to me was immediate. She attempted to hop down from the high stool she sat on but one of the officers placed his hand on her arm halting her movement.

"It's fine, Giselle."

I headed in her direction but Bennet's hand on my arm halted me.

"I'd prefer if you let her finish making her statement. I want to show you what we're dealing with here."

I paused and stared up at Detective Bennet. I fought the urge to order his hand off my arm. He was behaving oddly and I had a feeling that it was partly to do with the fact that he couldn't get in contact with Aaron. However, that wasn't my fault and I didn't want to simply stand by and let him upset me in an attempt to anger Aaron.

I glanced down at Arianna in the car seat I held. She looked so small, her tiny hands curled into fists as she slept.

"If you're about to take me to the body then I'd prefer if I could leave Arianna here with Giselle. I don't think a crime scene is the place for my daughter."

Bennet glanced down at the car seat for the first time since I'd arrived, the look of surprise on his face confusing me. He'd watched me carry her up the steps and into the warehouse, the last thing he should be is surprised that I didn't want to bring her into contact with a dead body.

"Of course…"

He trailed off as he gestured to the two officers that stood with Giselle. The moment he looked at them they immediately took a step away from the trembling Giselle. She hopped down from the stool she sat on as soon as she realised she was free to move around.

"Heather, it's awful there's so much…"

Bennet interrupted with a cough.

"Please don't share any of the details with Ms Ashcroft, I want all of this to be a…"

He paused as though struggling to find the right words.

"Surprise?"

I piped up shooting him a look of contempt as I handed Arianna over. She barely stirred in the car seat as Giselle took it and drew it in against her body. She held it as though merely being near to Arianna gave her comfort and perhaps it did. Whatever she had seen back there in the back room had left her in a state.

"That's not what I intended but I need you to look at the scene with fresh eyes. I need you to tell me if anything seems different."

His words piqued my curiosity and I nodded rather than answering him. I gave Arianna one last lingering look, I was reluctant to hand her over to anyone but it was better this way.

Bennet nodded at me as though trying to gauge whether I was truly on board with his plan.

"Let's get this over with."

He took off walking, his stride long and confidant as he crossed the warehouse and started down towards the storage areas at the back. I followed him, each step more hesitant than the last. My stomach churned and the sound of my heart beating in my ears drowned out everything else.

We reached the large metal doors at the back of the room, one of them was thrown wide open and the darkness that usually lay beyond was lit with a bright white light.

Men in uniforms and white protective clothing milled over and back inside the room.

"Can you all give us a moment?"

Bennet's voice brooked no argument and the people working within the room cast each other sidelong glances as they stood and emptied from the room. One of the uniformed officers remained standing near the door as Bennet stepped up to him.

"Did you hear me? I said I wanted a minute."

"I'm supposed to keep watch on the scene, make sure nothing is tampered with…"

"And I'm your superior, I've given you a direct order. Unless you want to find yourself demoted to traffic, get your ass out of here."

The cop hesitated for a moment but Bennet shot him one final hard look and the cop shrugged. He moved away from the room, trailing after the others who had started back towards the front of the warehouse.

Bennet stepped through the door and turned as though expecting me to be right behind him. Instead I stood a few feet back from the door. A shake had started in my hands and it was rapidly spreading through my body.

I was worried that once it reached my legs that they would cease holding me upright.

"You won't see anything back there."

Bennet's voice was soft and filled with an understanding that I didn't think he had.

"That's the point. Why are you showing me this?"

He studied me for a second and I watched the look of compassion slide out of his eyes. His face hardened as he stared at me and I knew that in a way he was punishing me because of Aaron but I had no idea why.

"I told you, I need you to tell me if anything seems out of place…"

"Cut the lies, Detective, you and I both know this has nothing to do with me noticing something new."

He cast a look over his shoulder into the room, his eyes flickering over the scene that only he could truly make out from his position in the doorway.

"I'm not going to force you in here, if you want to walk away then you're free to do so…"

"But?"

"But I watched you look into the box Hank delivered to your house. I watched the look on your face. You were horrified but you needed to see it, you needed to know the terrible thing he had done. It was almost as though you could learn from it… I don't know… Maybe I've completely misread you."

He fell silent and scrubbed his hand back over his short haircut. He closed his eyes and let his head drop back onto his shoulders. Tension flowed in every muscle in his body and I could tell that he was desperate to close the case. Desperate enough to do anything.

I stepped forward and touched his arm making him flinch. His eyes flew open and he stared down at me with a haunted look on his face.

"What has he done to you?"

My words came out as little more than a whisper but I knew he heard me, his eyes filled with horror as though whatever he had seen in my eyes was the most traumatic thing he could have witnessed.

Bennet's hand snaked out, his fingers closing around my upper arm as he jerked me forward and over the threshold. He continued to drag me forward and initially I fought him. I slapped at his hands but it was utterly pointless.

He pulled me into the centre of the room and it took my eyes a few moments to truly focus in on what I was looking at. There was an odd smell in the room almost coppery and I could taste it on the back of my tongue.

My eyes darted around, desperately trying to make sense of the dark thick syrupy puddle that had spread across the floor. In the light it looked almost black and as my eyes focused in on the source of the puddle I quickly realised that the fabric wrapped and lumpy shape was a person.

Instantly I closed my eyes. My brain struggling to put the pieces together... The place where the face should have been was gone, replaced with a ruined mess and the more I thought about it the more my stomach rebelled.

Jerking out of Bennet's grip I spun around, groping my way forward and out of the room. The moment I reached the main area of the warehouse I dropped to my knees and threw up.

My eyes streamed and my stomach rolled until there was nothing left inside me and still I continued to dry heave.

Bennet's worn brown shoes appeared in my eye line and he held a small tissue out to me. I didn't want to take it from him but I didn't have any myself. Snatching it from his grip I dabbed at my mouth and closed my eyes. Of course with my eyes closed the images from the fabric room instantly flooded back into my mind. It seemed even if I wasn't directly in front of it, there would be no escape from what I had come face to face with.

"Did you see it?"

Bennet spoke to me, his voice a little higher than usual. I pushed myself to my feet and faced him.

"You mean the body? Of course I saw the body, it was a little hard to miss after you dragged me in there."

He shook his head.

"No, you need to look at the wall."

He reached out to me again as though he was about to drag me back into the room but I shook my head and took a step back.

"I'm not going back in there."

"You have to see it…"

"Why? What the hell is so important about the wall that I 'have' to see it. It's enough that you dragged me in there and forced me to look at whoever that was…"

The look on Bennet's face became a little more manic and this time when he reached out for me I moved further from him and the room.

"I'm not going back in there, Detective."

He stepped towards me, his hand whipping out as he latched onto me. He drew me in against his body and I couldn't stop the scream that erupted from me. I fought against him, determined to not subject myself to any more nightmares.

His grip tightened on me as he picked me up from the ground and carried me back towards the room. I did the only thing I could do then, sealing my eyes shut against the sight I knew lay before me.

"Heather, you have to look… He'll know if you don't see it… He said he would know…"

Bennet's words surprised me but I didn't have the chance to question him. Strong arms wrapped around me, dragging me from Bennet's strangle hold. I opened my eyes in time to see the police officers that had swarmed into the room push him to his knees on the floor. He continued to fight against them, a desperation in his eyes that rattled me to my very core.

"Just look at it, please, just look at it!"

His voice was high and pitched with panic as he struggled to gesture to something on the wall behind me. There was something so utterly terrifying about his behaviour that against my better judgement I swivelled my head and stared at the back wall of the room.

My eyes wanted to drop down to the scene I knew lay on the floor but I fought the urge, keeping my eye line above the level.

The officer that held me, let me stand on my own two feet as he tried to direct me back towards the door but my eyes were suddenly glued to the wall.

Hank had gone to a lot of trouble to leave the body in here and I suddenly understood why. It was a message, it was all a message but how would Hank have known that I would come here, that I would see his message?

My eyes slid across the words and I was suddenly glad that there was nothing left in my stomach.

"Has he told you about the last night he worked with me? Has he told you how much he enjoyed the sound of her screams, the feel of her warm blood on his hands?"

Hank hadn't mentioned Aaron's name but I knew without a doubt that it was Aaron he meant. What I couldn't wrap my head around was what the hell he was talking about. It didn't make sense.

I dragged my gaze away from the wall and the message, my eyes falling on Bennet once more. He was suddenly quiet and utterly calm once more. He knelt on the floor as the other officers cuffed him and dragged him to his feet. A shiver of fear raced through me as I realised that everything he had done had been because Hank had made him.

No one could be trusted and if that was true then did that mean that I couldn't trust Aaron anymore?

I stumbled, my head suddenly swimming. I reached out, my hand closing on the arm of the officer that had pulled me from Bennet's grip.

"Please?"

It was the only word I could get out of my mouth before my eyes rolled back in my head and the darkness closed in around me. The thought of Aaron being someone I couldn't trust was too much to bear and the darkness swallowed me, blotting out the world and everything I knew in it. And in a way it was easier than dealing with the thoughts swirling in my mind.

Chapter Fifteen

AARON SAT IN THE BACK of the black SUV and stared out of the tinted windows. The inside of the car was filled with tension and the men gathered around him seemed to think that he would be the first one to break. But Aaron had played this game too many times in the past, they had come for him, they could be the ones to break the silence.

"Mr Ashcroft, where is McKinley?"

The one who had seemed to be in charge inside the prison was the first one to speak. He angled himself in the seat he sat in, his blue eyes piercing in their intensity. It was an intimidation tactic and one that might have worked on someone who was unfamiliar with the method.

"Hank has him."

The man sitting across from him stiffened slightly and Aaron could see the colour beneath his tan drain from his face leaving him with a sickly pallor.

"And you know this how?"

"He called me when I was at the prison. He knew I was going to be there… He wanted to tease me."

"Tease you?"

"That's probably the wrong word but it's the closest one I can think of. Hank enjoys what he's doing, to him the phone call he made is a tease, it's all a game as far as he's concerned."

The man with the blue eyes nodded thoughtfully and Aaron quickly realised that he had no idea that McKinley was dead.

"Are you going to give me your name? You do after all have me at a disadvantage, you know my name, I don't know yours."

"I'm Forester. I was Mr Wells' handler before he dropped all contact."

"So why didn't you come sooner? Why didn't you come when I told you what he was capable of, when I warned you of what he seemed to be ramping up towards."

Forester sighed, his expression growing colder as he contemplated what to say. Aaron knew if he thought he could get away with it that he would lie and Aaron wasn't interested in hearing a pretty but utterly concocted story.

"Save the lies, I want straight answers, at this point I think I deserve them."

Aaron shifted uncomfortably in the seat he sat in, his ribs continued to ache and each breath was growing more and more painful. He needed painkillers, the only problem was that the really good ones dulled his responses and he couldn't afford that. Not until Hank was safely out of the picture.

"Fine, we had an arrangement with Mr Wells and as long as he continued to check in with us and followed orders when they were given to him, he was afforded certain luxuries…"

Aaron shook his head as though the movement could help him understand the words he had just heard a little better. There had to be a mistake, it wasn't possible that Forester had just said what he thought he had.

"You're going to have to repeat that, I think I misunderstood you."

Forester sighed again but this time it wasn't a happy sound. He dropped his gaze to the floor of the SUV and for a second Aaron was almost certain that he saw a flicker of doubt pass through his eyes.

"You didn't misunderstand, Mr Ashcroft."

Aaron laughed, the sound leaving his mouth in a harsh bark. It hurt to laugh but he couldn't help it, the sound escaped him, the sheer ridiculousness of the situation overwhelming him.

"You're telling me that you already knew what Hank was up to… That you just turned a blind eye to it as long as he did your dirty work?"

"Mr Wells was a valuable asset, indulging his private business seemed like the best way to keep him on track. Everything was always monitored and where possible life was preserved but..."

"But what? You let a monster do whatever in hell he wanted to do in order to keep him on a leash? Are you mad? You're supposed to be the good guys... You're supposed to protect people from the likes of Hank."

Forester shook his head and lifted his gaze back up to meet Aaron's.

"I assure you, Mr Wells' odd slips were in the interest of keeping people safe. He was very good at his job and he saved far more lives than he ever..."

One of the other men sitting in the front of the SUV coughed suddenly and Aaron knew it was an attempt to stop Forester from spilling too much information. They still wouldn't ever admit to the part they played in it all.

"Murdered, you can say it, he murdered people and you let him."

"That's not what happened."

"You created him, you recruited him knowing what he was and then you gave him as much power as he wanted..."

"We didn't create him, we used his distinct abilities to our advantage, there is a difference. We recruited you to keep him in check and it worked until now..."

Aaron sat back against his seat, the air suddenly sucked out of his lungs at Forester's words.

"What?"

Forester smiled but it wasn't a friendly look. Clearly he didn't like to be questioned and Aaron was good at questioning authority, for too long he had watched it corrupt those around him. But this, what Forester had just admitted to, this was something different.

"You heard me. Your job was to keep, Hank Wells in check, and you did your job admirably until you left…"

"I left because I had to, my injuries…"

"Your injuries were something you could have come back from, you chose not to. You knew what Hank was, you knew what he was capable of, Aaron, and yet you still walked away from all of that."

Aaron shook his head, Forester's words were like tiny razor blades. They slid beneath his skin opening him up, leaving him vulnerable. If he was to believe Forester then all of this was his fault. Aaron had spent years carrying guilt but this wasn't something he was willing to carry.

"No one told me I was hired as a personal nanny but then I wouldn't expect you to tell me anything straight."

"I assure you, Aaron, that I'm not lying. I think it's important that everyone knows exactly what's going on. It wouldn't be fair for one side to hold all the cards."

Shock ricocheted through Aaron as it dawned on him what Forester was trying to tell him.

"I'm not the only one who knows the truth am I? Hank knows this too…"

The pieces slowly started to fall into place. Hank's recent behaviour, the way he had suddenly switched and started targeting people that Aaron cared about. He knew what Aaron had been hired to do… Hank probably even believed that he knew the truth too.

"We have reason to believe that Hank is aware…"

"How could you let him do this? I have a family to look after, how could you just let him come after me?"

Aaron pushed out of the seat and rammed Forester back against the head rest, his hands balling up in Forester's shirt.

"He's taken Kirsty, a complete innocent in all of this…"

Forester broke Aaron's hold, his movements fast and decisive as he pushed Aaron back into his own seat once more.

"I'm more than aware of what he's done, why do you think we're here?"

"I don't think you care about Kirsty. I don't think you care about me or the people I love. I think you're only here because you want to know what happened to McKinley."

"He was supposed to contact you and formulate a plan to get Hank back on course."

"He's dead."

Aaron spat the words out. He felt bad for McKinley and although he might not have liked the man, he certainly would never have wished death at the hands of Hank.

"Dead? How can you be certain?"

Forester sounded genuinely shocked and Aaron felt a small flicker of happiness within himself to know that he could still surprise men like Forester.

Aaron watched as he turned and whispered to the man sitting in the front of the car. There was a lot of nodding before Forester turned back in his seat and levelled his barely contained rage squarely on Aaron.

"How can you possibly know that for certain?"

"I told you, Hank called me, he had McKinley and he wanted to know if we were allies. Hank simply did what Hank does best and I was forced to listen as he shot him."

"And you didn't think any of this was important? You didn't think you should mention it to me?"

The SUV started forward, the wheels squealing on the asphalt as it pulled out into the flow of traffic. The sudden movement momentarily threw Aaron back against the seat and he winced as pain flared through his body once more.

"Sir, it's not a lie, they've found a body and it seems to match McKinley."

One of the men sitting in the front of the SUV swivelled in his seat as much as they belt he wore would allow and addressed Forester over his shoulder. Aaron watched as the man sitting in front of him, who had just moments before appeared so calm, suddenly switch. Colour flared up through his face and his eyes sparked with the anger he felt.

"I will find a way to hold you personally responsible for this."

Forester's voice was tight and Aaron could tell from the way he curled his fists that he meant every word he said.

"And I promise you this, if Hank hurts any of the people in my life I will hold you responsible and you don't want me holding you responsible for anything."

The tension rose as the SUV rounded the corner and pulled up outside a warehouse that Aaron recognised only too well. His heart plummeted in his chest instantly. If Hank was trying to send a message then Aaron had received it loud and clear.

The moment the SUV pulled to a halt Aaron was out and moving up towards the main doors. Heather's car was parked in front of the building a cold fist of fear had punched its way through to his gut.

The police officer standing in front of the yellow tape barrier instantly raised his hand as though he could stop Aaron from slipping beneath. But Heather was here somewhere and no one would keep Aaron from her.

"Sir, you can't come in here."

The cop stepped up to him as Aaron ducked beneath the barrier and started to move towards the front steps.

"My wife is in there…"

"Sir, I can't…"

The police officer trailed off as Forester stepped up to the line and pulled his badge from the inside of his jacket pocket.

"Special Agent Forester, Mr Ashcroft there is with us…"

The cop instantly let his hand drop away from Aaron's arm and turned his full attention to Forester. It was all the distraction Aaron needed and he wasted no time in striding to the steps and up into the warehouse.

The moment he stepped inside the door he saw Giselle Heather's assistant. She sat inside the doors with Arianna cradled tightly in her arms.

"Where's Heather?"

Aaron's voice came out far harsher than he intended and as soon as Giselle tilted her head up to look at him with large tear filled eyes he instantly felt bad. She hiccuped and dipped her face back down to Arianna's head.

"She went to view the body with one of the detectives…"

"What?"

Aaron couldn't keep the shock from his voice. It didn't make sense. Why the hell would Heather have gone to see the body? What could she possibly know about the situation that might help the cops to catch Hank?

Giselle started to repeat her words but Aaron didn't wait for her to finish. The sound of a scream erupted from the back of the warehouse and Aaron instantly recognised it as Heather's voice. He'd have known the sound of her voice anywhere and to hear fear in it filled him with dread.

Aaron started towards the back of the warehouse at a dead run. He passed the empty tables covered in designs and bolts of fabric, sliding between the desks in an attempt to get to her.

He wasn't the only one who had heard the scream and as he reached the back of the warehouse he caught sight of the cops that were flooding into one of the storage rooms. He followed them in and came face to face with Heather as she collapsed into the arms of one of the officers.

"Heather?"

Her eyes were closed and she lay across the arms of the officer as her legs went from beneath her. Aaron darted forward, catching her before the cop even had a chance to properly realise what was happening.

"What happened?"

Aaron's voice was filled with panic as he pulled her against his chest. His ribs ached viciously but none of it mattered, not when he held Heather unconscious in his grip.

The cop shrugged and looked a little lost as Aaron swept Heather up into his arms. It was then he caught sight of the body propped against the shelving units. Hank had wrapped McKinley in a large piece of fabric, however, he had been sure to leave what was left of the man's head unwrapped for everyone to see.

Aaron started to turn but the sight of something plastered across the walls in red caught his attention.

"Has he told you about the last night he worked with me? Has he told you how much he enjoyed the sound of her screams, the feel of her warm blood on his hands?"

It was Hank's writing and Aaron's heart came to a shuddering halt as he realised the words were meant for Heather.

He carried her from the room, holding her against his body until she began to stir softly.

"Heather, what happened? Are you alright?"

He kept his voice low, cautious as he held her. Her eyes fluttered open and the minute she stared up at him, her gaze instantly filled with fear and confusion.

"Aaron, what does he mean? The message he left, what does it mean?"

Her voice was fearful as she struggled to push away from him but he held onto her. He wasn't about to let Hank come between them, not now, not when they had already gotten through so much.

"Heather, it's a lie, it's all a lie. He'll say anything to rip us apart because that's what he wants."

"But, Aaron..."

She trailed off for a second and dropped her gaze to the floor. Aaron slid his fingers beneath her chin and tilted her head up.

"Heather, what is it?"

She stared at him, her eyes filled with sorrow and fear. Aaron hated to think that he might have put the look in her eyes and he hated Hank even more for what he had caused.

"The nightmares..."

"Nightmares?"

Aaron stared at her with confusion and shook his head. What did nightmares have to do with any of this? Was she trying to tell him that she had dreamt of the terrible things Hank had done?

"Your nightmares, the ones that wake you in the middle of the night. You think I don't hear anything but I know about them. I've listened to what you've said in your sleep and now suddenly it all makes sense…"

"You know about the nightmares?"

Aaron released Heather and took a trembling step backwards. He watched her nod and his heart sank in his chest.

"I thought they were just dreams, that Hank had affected you, he was your friend and then he…"

She trailed off as though she was unable to continue with her own sentence. She glanced past him, her eyes raking over the doorway beyond where they stood as though she could still see the body that lay within the room.

"The things he says I've done, they're lies, Heather, I'm not like him, I've never been like him."

"But you don't remember what happened, you don't remember what happened… Aaron what if he's telling the truth?"

Aaron opened his mouth to answer her but it felt as though someone had punched a hole through his chest. How could Heather think that about him? How could she believe someone like Hank over him, over the man she claimed to love?

"I know enough about that night, Heather, to know I'm not like Hank. Whatever happened that night wasn't the way Hank has portrayed it. His is a twisted set of events."

"Aaron…"

She reached out to him but Aaron shrugged away from her. The thought that she believed Hank over him was almost too much to bear and it was the last thing that he expected. But could he blame her? He was the one having the nightmares and they terrified him... Was it possible that in his sleep he had spoken the truth of that night?

He started towards the main doors of the warehouse once more and Heather followed him. The moment her hand reached for him, Aaron pulled away from her grip once more and continued to the doors. He could feel her eyes on him as he walked away but he still didn't look back.

His cell phone buzzed in his pocket and as he scooped it out he didn't recognise the phone number displayed across the screen. Pressing the call answer button Aaron half expected to hear Hank's gleeful tone on the other end of the line.

"Mr Ashcroft?"

The voice seemed familiar but it definitely wasn't Hank and for that Aaron was instantly relieved.

"Yes, who is this?"

"This is Warden Silas Granger, you were in my prison a mere few hours ago, I need you to come back."

Aaron laughed but it wasn't a pleasant sound and it wasn't intended as one.

"You must be crazy, Warden. Not so long ago you were accusing me of plotting to kill one of your inmates, why would I do anything you want?"

Silence followed Aaron's words and for a moment he questioned whether he was still connected to the Warden's call. The emptiness was finally broken by the sound of the warden sighing.

"There was an attempt made on Mr Fossen's life, we don't know whether he will survive it or not."

Granger's words shocked Aaron. He knew it was foolish to be surprised by any of the events unfolding and yet he still was.

"Hank did this..."

"Mr Fossen had a plan in place in case of something like this occurring. I'm merely carrying it out, Mr Ashcroft, he wants to see you."

"I thought you said you didn't know if he would even make it?"

"He was very clear, Mr Ashcroft, he wishes to speak with you. He has refused to go in for surgery until he speaks with you. He says he has information you want."

It was all Aaron needed to hear.

"Where is he?"

"He's currently down in the hospital prison wing at Memorial."

Aaron didn't wait for Granger to say anything else. Instead he hung up, closing the phone and pushing it back into his pocket as he came face to face with Forester.

"You want Hank? Then get me over to Memorial, the prison wing and let me speak to the only person who knows what Hank has in mind."

"And if I don't?"

"Then the only one who knows where Hank is will die and he'll slip through our fingers again, McKinley's death will have been for nothing."

Forester hesitated before finally nodding and heading for the steps outside the door. Aaron paused and glanced back over his shoulder. Heather stood with Giselle, he could tell from the tension in her shoulders that she was upset but there was nothing he could do until he had brought Hank down. Aaron followed Forester out through the doors and down the steps. He climbed into the back of the van alongside Forester and all he could see in his mind was Heather's face and the look of fear in her eyes. He would do whatever it took to take that look from her face. No matter the cost.

Chapter Sixteen

*S*ITTING IN THE CAR ON the drive home I couldn't help but feel guilty. The look of betrayal in Aaron's eyes when I had told him that I knew about his dreams... He hadn't waited for me to explain, maybe if he had it wouldn't feel as though an unfixable rift had opened up between us.

Hank's words bothered me. I didn't honestly believe that what he had written was the truth. I knew Aaron and although the words had surprised me it didn't change the fact that deep down I knew what Aaron was capable of and it wasn't what Hank had accused him of. No, Hank's words bothered me because most of what Hank spoke of stemmed from a place of truth. And if that was the case then it meant that Aaron had a secret past, something he hadn't shared with me or even attempted to share with me.

LOVING THE BILLIONAIRE EVER AFTER

I pulled into the driveway of the house, the darkness surprising me. With the doubling of the security that Aaron had insisted on the house was always bright and it was never empty.

I pulled the car to a halt outside and stared up at the darkened windows, my heart skittering around in my chest.

The events of the evening had spooked me and I gave myself a mental shake in an attempt to get rid of the uneasiness that had settled in my gut. Arianna stirred in her seat in the back of the car, a small cry escaping her.

Hunger.

I knew her cry and it was instantly recognisable. It was all I needed to shed the last of my uneasy feelings from looking up at a darkened house. Climbing from the car I hurried to the back door. It didn't take long to unbuckle her seat and lift her clear of the car. Silence had settled over the open expanse of land that surrounded me, nothing stirred.

Arianna started to cry once more, her sobs becoming more and more insistent with every minute I wasted standing outside. Fishing the keys out of my bag I carried her up the steps onto the wrap around porch and pushed the door open.

The moment I stepped inside the tell tale beep of the alarm system started up and mingled with the cries of Arianna. Placing her seat on the floor I entered the security code and waited for the system to recognise the command. It responded instantly and the downstairs lights flickered on automatically.

It amazed me that Aaron had managed to find a system that could do so much and was so utterly intuitive. I scooped Arianna up once more and started for the kitchen. The sound of footsteps on the stairs surprised me. I reacted, scooping Arianna from her car seat and moving quickly and quietly towards the door to the kitchen, Arianna's small hiccuping sobs making it difficult to hear anything untoward.

"Heather?"

Carrie's voice filtered through the hall and I released a long sigh of relief. I stepped out from my place in the shadow near the door and smiled.

"You scared the hell out of me."

Carrie sheepishly grinned and headed towards me.

"I scared you? When I heard the alarm beeping I didn't know what to think. It was that little cutie there that gave you away."

She gestured towards Arianna who was now beginning to wind herself up into a proper tantrum. Grinning I moved into the kitchen and Carrie followed just behind me.

"Where are the security guards?"

I said to Carrie as I shifted Arianna in my grip and glanced over at her.

"I don't know. They were here with David before I went up for a lie down. When David got a phone call from Aaron asking him to come and meet him, he got ready and I didn't come back down."

Curiosity got the best of me.

"Did he say why he had to go and meet him?"

She shook her head, "he wouldn't say why but it seemed pretty serious."

I shot her a look over my shoulder as I began to prepare a bottle for Arianna. Carrie moved up beside me and reached out.

"I'll take her while you do that."

I nodded and let her take the tiny wriggling bundle from my arms. I didn't question her about the call David had received from his brother, if she knew anything then I knew she would tell me. No doubt the boys were probably trying to keep everything under wraps in a misguided attempt to protect us.

From the corner of my eye I watched Carrie carefully as she cooed and hummed a soothing lullaby that seemed to calm Arianna down. It was then I noticed the bump that was beginning to show beneath the t-shirt she wore.

"You're starting to show."

She looked up at me a startled but happy look on her face.

"I thought maybe the doctor was exaggerating today when I went in for the scan."

"You had your scan?"

I picked the bottle up and tested the temperature of the milk against my skin. Carrie nodded and I could see the glint of excitement in her eyes.

"Well? What did they say? Did you ask about the sex of the baby?"

She grinned and nodded.

"Yeah, David wasn't sure if he wanted to know but I couldn't wait for months to find out."

She paused and I reached over taking Arianna from her arms. Picking up the bottle I placed the bottle to her lips and waited for her to start feeding. She caught it immediately, her tiny hands catching the bottle as though she could draw it closer to her face.

"Are you going to tell me or do I have to guess."

I smiled back at her as I moved over to the kitchen table and took a seat.

"We're having a boy. When David heard the news he was a little stunned, I'm not sure what he expected."

I started to laugh momentarily startling Arianna who jerked in my arms, a small mewl escaping her as the bottle slipped. I could imagine David's face, I could still remember the look on Aaron's face when he'd come face to face with our daughter and it wasn't something I would ever forget.

Arianna came to the end of her bottle and I set it back down on the kitchen counter before I started to wind her. She curled her small hands into fists, the grumpy expression she wore reminded me of Aaron whenever he was forced to do something he didn't want to do. That thought alone made me smile.

"I started looking at names, I know it's still too soon but I just couldn't help myself. I'll show you the ones I have marked out."

She started out into the hall and I stood to follow her.

"Bring it into Arianna's room, I need to change her and get her ready for bed."

Carrie nodded as she moved up the stairs ahead of me. Arianna grumbled quietly in my arms as I carried her up the stairs and down the hall to the nursery. I pushed open the door and fumbled in the darkness for the light switch.

The door thumped closed behind me and I jumped as my fingers finally found the light switch.

"I was wondering how long it would take you to get upstairs."

Hank's voice sent icy shivers racing down my back and I fought to keep my fear in check.

He leaned against the door and lifted his hand, letting his fingers trail down across my cheek. Shrugging away from him I pressed Arianna more securely in against my body, shielding her from his sight.

"What the hell are you doing here? If you touch me, Aaron will kill you."

I hissed my words out from between my teeth. I didn't want to disturb Arianna too much but I also didn't want to draw Carrie to the room. I'd told her to come and meet me in here but as I stood near the door I prayed that something else took her attention.

"I'm counting on Aaron coming after me. I thought taking Kirsty would be enough to draw him out but now I know the truth... You're the real reason he's gone soft, you and that pathetic bag of blood and flesh you're clutching against your chest."

Shock rocketed through me as I quickly realised he was talking about Arianna. He truly had no empathy left within him and I knew begging and pleading with a man like this would serve no purpose. Even Jude could be reasoned with, his proclivities tended towards the sadistic but he enjoyed watching the emotion and pain he could inflict on others. Hank was different, he didn't care how others felt as long as it was something he enjoyed.

"If you touch her Aaron won't be the only one you'll have to worry about. I'll kill you myself."

My words left me in a blaze of fury and Arianna stirred in my grip. Hank started to laugh as he took a step towards me. His movement took him away from his position against the door.

"You won't be fit to do anything once I start chopping little pieces off you."

Hank's voice was actually filled with happiness and it sickened me to my very stomach.

The door flopped open with enough force to ram him into the middle of the room. Carrie's wide frightened eyes met mine as she stood framed in the doorway. I didn't wait for Hank to recover, my legs kicking into action as they carried me forward and out into the hall.

I pushed Carrie forward, propelling her toward the bedroom I shared with Aaron. We could have tried for the stairs but with Arianna in my arms and Carrie pregnant the risk of tripping or Hank catching up to us was far too great.

His roar of frustration echoed through the house making my heart jump in my chest.

Carrie stumbled ahead of me and into the bedroom.

"The minute I heard you talking to him I tried the phone in the hall but the line is dead... He cut the lines, Heather!"

I propped Arianna on the expanse of patterned blanket the covered the king size bed before I raced over to the dresser.

A loud crack and the sound of splintering wood told me Hank was coming.

I glanced out into the hall as I rammed the door shut, catching sight of him as he trundled down the hall towards us.

My hands shook as I rammed the lock home, securing the door against his onslaught but I knew it wouldn't keep him out for long.

"Carrie, help me with the dresser."

She stood watching me with wide frightened eyes, shock freezing her in place.

"Carrie!"

She jerked into motion, grabbing one side of the heavy wooden piece of furniture. Wrapping my hands around the opposite side I pulled, tension sang through my body as we struggled to make it budge across the floor.

Glancing over at Arianna on the bed gave me the strength I needed. If Hank got in here... The things he would do to the people I loved didn't bear thinking about.

"Carrie, push. We can't let him get in here... Think of the baby."

I watched her grit her teeth, tears dripping down her cheeks as she pushed harder and the dresser started to move.

Hank's body collided with the door, or at least I presumed it was his body. He flung himself against the wood with enough force to rattle the door in its frame.

"Is this really what you want, Heather? Hiding from me only makes me angrier, just imagine what I'll do to your brat and the pregnant bitch once I get in there."

His voice was low and frightening and it wasn't just the pressure of moving the dresser that was making me shake. But his words only made me more determined to stop him from getting into the room. I wasn't about to let anything happen to Arianna or Carrie.

With one final shove we managed to get the heavy wooden piece of furniture in front of the door. I turned and watched as Carrie backed slowly away from the door, the fear in her eyes making her look very young and vulnerable.

Hank crashed against the door once more and it felt as though the entire house shook. We both jumped and Arianna started to cry.

If we could wait it out then the security guards would come. They had to know something was wrong... Aaron would know something was wrong...

LOVING THE BILLIONAIRE EVER AFTER

How? You basically told him you think he's as bad as the monster trying to crash through the door. He won't be back to save you.

The small voice in the back of my mind sent all hope of a rescue scuttling from my mind. It was true, the things I had said to Aaron were unforgivable.

An idea hit me, Aaron had a gun safe hidden in the back of the closet. He'd shared the combination with me in case anything ever happened. Scrambling over to the closet I popped the door open and pushed aside the clothes and shoes that were haphazardly arranged in front of it. I didn't have to reach the safe to know something was wrong, I could already tell from the mess that lay in the bottom of the closet.

The electronic pad that normally sat on the front of the safe was now a melted mess of wires and metal.

Hank had thought of everything. If he'd had enough time to plan ahead cut the phone lines and take care of the gun safe in the off chance that I might try to use a gun, then there was no security guards going to come to the rescue. They were probably hurt or worse, dead.

The sound of splintering wood sent my heart rate skittering through the roof. There was no way to keep him out, no way to prevent him from hurting the ones I loved... Or was there?

Standing, I walked over to the bed and lifted Arianna from her place on the blanket. I hugged her to my body, burying my face in against her, drinking in her soft baby scent.

There was so much I wanted to say, so much I wanted to tell her but there wasn't enough time for any of it.

Instead I handed her over to Carrie and pushed them both towards the en-suite door.

"Hide, you have to hide. Lock the door and don't you dare come out of there, no matter what happens."

Carrie's hand found mine, her fingers wrapping around my wrist as she tried to pull me into the bathroom after her. But I knew there was no way out. If I could buy her enough time I would, Hank was here for me after all. Carrie and Arianna just needed time and if I could give it to them then it would all be worth while.

"Heather, you can hide with us, please, don't do this."

I shook my head and smiled at her.

"Keep, Arianna safe, keep your boy safe and I promise you I'll be alright."

It was a lie, I had no idea if I would make it out of this alive but I had to protect Arianna and Carrie was completely innocent in all of this. She didn't deserve to be hurt because of me.

I pushed her into the bathroom as the wooden frame of the bedroom door shook and splintered again. The dresser that sat in front of it crashed to the ground and I closed my eyes as Hank broke pieces of the door away.

"Carrie, please."

I pleaded with her, there was no time left and we were out of options.

She nodded and slammed the door shut. I listened as the bolt slid home, locking her and Arianna safely within.

I moved into the middle of the room, the faint sound of Arianna's cries in my ears as I waited for Hank to finish his complete destruction of the door.

I wasn't afraid, it was probably stupid and maybe it was just shock that was keeping my fear at bay. But in that moment as I waited for him to come and get me I felt utterly calm. I had done everything I could to protect Arianna. As long as she was safe then nothing else truly mattered. Nothing Hank could do to me or threaten me with would be as terrifying or painful as long as she was alright. Reaching down to the floor I scooped up one of the pieces of wood that had broken away from the door. Hefting it in my hands I tested what it would feel like to use as a weapon.

The final piece of the door broke apart and I could suddenly see him. My fear came back to me in a rush the moment I saw the smile on his face.

"I'm going to enjoy this."

His words shook me to the core and as he stepped through the broken door I lifted the bit of wood I held in my hands and prepared to defend what was mine.

Chapter Seventeen

AARON STOOD OUTSIDE THE HOSPITAL room of the one man he had always believed he would rejoice the death of. Instead he waited to speak to him, hoping against hope that Jude would know something he could use against Hank.

"Have you seen him yet?"

David said as he stalked up the corridor.

Aaron shook his head and dropped back against the wall.

"No they want to stabilise him but the only way to do that is surgery, which Jude won't allow because he's worried he'll die on the table."

"This is ridiculous, if they keep everything held up then he will die on the table."

David sounded furious and at any other time Aaron might have found it funny. But right now he couldn't.

Hank had already killed McKinley and the message he'd left for Heather suggested he had something far worse in mind.

The door to Jude's room opened slowly and one of the doctor's Aaron had seen hurrying in moments before David had arrived appeared.

"Can I speak to him now?"

Aaron didn't wait for the man to shut the door before approaching him.

"And you are?"

"I'm the one he wants to see, I'm the reason he refuses to go down to surgery."

The doctor shook his head, the look on his face grim.

"Mr Fossen is slipping in and out of consciousness, the time for surgery has passed and all we can do now is make the time he has left as comfortable as possible."

Aaron took a step forward.

"I need to speak to him, he has information I…"

The doctor raised his hand silencing Aaron.

"I don't think you heard me. Mr Fossen is in no fit state to receive visitors aside from those of his family and that will only happen when we have him sufficiently comfortable."

"You need to let me in there, I don't think you understand what's at stake here. That man lying in there is a murderer, he doesn't deserve to be comfortable and he has information I need, a young woman's life depends on it."

"He is my patient, it doesn't matter what he has done I'll treat him how I see fit."

The doctor turned and Aaron started after him but the sound of his phone buzzing in his pocket stopped him. Reaching into his jacket Aaron scooped it out and flipped it open pressing the small plastic device to his ear.

The muffled sound of screaming and Hank's excited laughter made Aaron's blood run cold.

"Leave, Kirsty alone, Hank, when I find you I'm going to kill you."

Hank's manic giggling increased but the words he spoke through his laughter stopped Aaron's heart in his chest.

"It's not Kirsty, Aaron. Don't tell me you don't recognise the panicked screams of your own wife. Hear, have a proper listen."

Something shifted and suddenly Aaron's senses were overwhelmed with the sobbing of Heather's frightened sobs.

"Heather?"

"Aaron, I'm sorry I did it to keep her safe, I'm so sorry…"

The phone went dead leaving Aaron holding it as the incessant beeping of the dead line droned in his ear.

"Heather…"

He uttered her name again shock robbing him of all sense. None of it seemed real. It had to be a dream, some sick nightmare that he would wake up from and once he did he would roll over in the bed and Heather would be there, safe beside him.

Regrets swirled in his mind. If he had stayed with her, if he had gone home with her she would be safe…

"Aaron, what's wrong?"

David's panicked shouts finally made it through the ringing in Aaron's ears.

"He has her, Hank has her…"

David shook his head and took a step back as though the thought of it was too much.

"How? I mean, it's not possible, is it?"

Aaron didn't answer his brother, there was no point, he didn't have the answers. There was one man who did have them though and Aaron intended to get them out of him, no matter what he had to do.

He strode to the hospital door and rammed it open. The heavy door flopped back against the wall and Aaron was vaguely aware of the sound of cracking plaster but he didn't care. None of it mattered.

"Where is she? Where has he taken her?"

The doctors and nurses gathered in the room looked shocked many of them opting to simply move out of Aaron's way. One of the doctor's who stepped up to him and placed his hand on Aaron's arm quickly found himself writhing on the floor, the hand he had used to try and stop Aaron with was bent at an awkward angle.

Reaching the bed Aaron leaned down over Jude, drains and tubes poked out of him and his face was practically unrecognisable beneath the swollen black and blue bruising.

"You wanted me here because you knew what he was planning. You knew as soon as he made a move against you that he planned on taking Heather. So tell me where he is... Tell me!"

Aaron shook Jude, his anger overwhelming him as he stared down into the broken face of someone who had made his life hell. How could it have come to this? How could something so important be left in the hands of someone so twisted?

"Does he have her?"

Jude's voice was marred by a strange wheeze that seemed to come from the very depths of his being.

"He's taken her but you already knew that. Now where is he, where has he taken her?"

"She's mine, he can't have her. He promised he would only end you."

Aaron grabbed the front of Jude's ripped shirt and jerked him up off the bed. His body felt strange, as though there were more bones inside it than he should have had. He moved upwards with Aaron, a strange gurgling sound escaping him as blood trickled from his mouth.

"Tell me where she is!"

Aaron pressed his face as close to Jude's as he could, staring into the other man's blood shot eyes.

"House, West Morton, it was one of my old properties..."

Jude's voice slurred off as blood bubbled up between his lips. It wasn't red, Aaron noted as security barrelled into him, dragging him away from Jude's bed. The bright blood had mixed with Jude's saliva, coating his teeth in an odd pink colour.

The sound of the machines screaming violently suddenly had Aaron realising that Jude was dying. Security bundled Aaron from the room as Jude jerked violently up and down on the bed.

Aaron was dumped out into the hall and the door slammed behind him. He couldn't deny the small feeling of satisfaction he had knowing that Jude wouldn't ever be an issue. That his time torturing women had come to an end. But all of that was destroyed by the knowledge that someone far worse than Jude had Heather and if he didn't act fast everything he had worked and fought for would be ripped away from him.

Chapter Eighteen

THE ROPE BOUND AROUND MY wrists chaffed against my skin and the cramped dark trunk of the car reeked of oil and something else, something I couldn't quite put my finger on and I wasn't even sure I wanted to.

The car turned again, the movement sending me sliding back against the metal boxes Hank had stuffed me in here with. I struggled to remember all the twists and turns the car had taken. If I had the opportunity then I would escape but I'd need to know where I was and how to get away.

The tyres crunched over a dirt road, the rocks and stones we passed over bouncing the car and me around like a rag doll. I could hear Hank, his voice practically hoarse as he crooned along to some song that had come on the radio. The thought of him happy made me sick. It didn't seem right that someone as twisted as he was could even be so happy. I would have done anything to wipe the smile from his face.

The car rolled to a stop and I grunted as one of the metal boxes slid into me with enough force to drive the air from my lungs. I pushed back against it in an attempt to make more room for myself in the trunk but it was pointless.

The sound of Hank's boots crunching across gravel sent my heart rate racing in my chest. I could hear my blood as it pumped in my ears, growing louder with each step that took him closer. I didn't want him to open the trunk, I didn't want to stare up into his face or watch the smile I knew he wore spread across his lips. Of course what I wanted didn't matter.

Hank popped the trunk open and stared down at me.

"I hope you weren't too uncomfortable in there."

He smiled, knowing full well how cramped a space it actually was.

I refused to answer him, there was no point in saying anything he seemed to get a kick out of everything that left my mouth.

He reached in grabbing the rope that bound my wrists, jerking me up with enough force to practically pull my arms from their sockets. A small gasp escaped me the pain surprising as he dragged me from the trunk of the car.

Once he had me out he stood in front of me close enough that every time he took a breath his chest touched my arm.

"You don't look different from any other girl on the street and yet, you're the girl that so many men would give up their lives for. What makes you special?"

He moved around me as he spoke, his words making me want to lash out. Instead, I struggled to hold everything in. I didn't want to give him any satisfaction, he'd taken enough from me when he'd made me beg back at the house.

Simply knowing Arianna was safe made it worthwhile but it didn't change the fact that it wasn't natural to beg a sadist like Hank to do whatever he wanted to me, as long as he would leave Arianna and Carrie alone in the bathroom.

His hand whipped out, his fingers wrapping into my hair as he jerked my head back exposing my neck. He moved closer, staring down into my face as though by studying me he could understand whatever it was he was struggling with.

I gritted my teeth, determined not to whimper. I didn't want to give him the satisfaction of knowing that what he was doing was painful.

"Why is Fossen so obsessed with you? Did you know he made me promise not to touch you… The things he had planned for you once he got out."

Hank smiled as though he were honestly reminiscing on a fond memory.

"Jude, wasn't going to get out, there was too much evidence against him…"

I squeezed the words out from between my lips, the pain from the grip he had on my hair and scalp filling my eyes with tears that I struggled to blink away.

"Oh, he knew he wouldn't get out legally but he had a plan… Really I did you a favour, it's just a pity you won't live long enough to enjoy it."

"You think by killing me instead of allowing Jude to kill me that you're somehow doing me a favour? You're more delusional than I thought."

Hank's face darkened, something in my words had made him angry. He dipped his head to mine pressing his face against my face as though he could become one with me through proximity.

"I'm not delusional, Heather, I just don't see the point in not having what I want. I'm very good at what I do, the government wouldn't have hired me if they didn't think so."

He buried his face in against my neck inhaling sharply and making me squirm. My movement only made him hold me tighter, crushing me against him. If it had been Jude holding me this close I would have thought it sexual but with Hank it wasn't. He was simply the predator and I was his prey.

He bit down on my shoulder hard enough to make me scream. Tears filled my eyes and spilled down my cheeks as he continued to bite down on me, like a dog who had caught a rabbit.

He released me and I collapsed against him, pain radiated from the place where he had sank his teeth into me and I could feel something warm and wet beginning to slide across my skin.

"Jude isn't an issue anymore, he was too much of a distraction for Aaron anyway."

"I don't understand?"

I sucked in a shaky breath through my teeth, the skin on my neck stinging and aching. Hank reached up and ran his fingers around the place where he had bitten me, the pain from something so simple had me fighting to keep my whimpers under control.

"He's dead, there can be no loose ends."

Hank didn't wait to see what my reaction would be. His hand wrapped around my arm and he jerked me forward toward the large house he had parked in front of.

His words filled me with dread, clearly where Hank was concerned there was no honour among thieves. If he had killed Jude in prison, I knew without a doubt that if he got me inside the house then I was never coming out.

I feigned a faint, dropping my body completely against him. It was enough to take him by surprise and his grip loosened on my arm just long enough for me to get into position. I turned in his grip, drawing my knee suddenly up in front of me as I drove it up into his crotch.

He grunted and crumpled forward towards me. He windmilled with his arms in an attempt to grab me but his movements were completely uncoordinated. I didn't wait for him to recover, I turned and sprinted down the drive. My shoes crunched over the gravel as I ran, I didn't look back my drive to escape pushing me forward. Escape was the only thing I knew as the air in my lungs burned.

Two small darts bit into my back, one between my shoulders and the other over my lower back. Pain sliced into me driving me to the ground. I went down face first into the dirt, my body convulsing as pain continued to rip through me.

Seconds passed but to me it felt more like hours. It took me a few moments to become aware of the crunch of Hank's boots on the gravel. I tried to move but my body wasn't interested in obeying me.

He crouched down next to me and the taser came into view. I watched through tear filled eyes as he disconnected the cartridge and dropped it onto the ground.

"You shouldn't have done that, Heather."

He pressed the exposed metal pins on the end of the taser into my neck and the world went black as searing pain ripped into me.

My mouth tasted of blood and dirt as I struggled to open my eyes. The back of my neck burned and my head swam as I lifted my head. I sat in the corner of what looked to have once been the kitchen of the house.

My vision was blurred and I shook my head in the hopes that I could clear it, all that did was make the pounding my skull much worse.

Something stirred and moaned.

I froze, the sound hadn't come from me and couldn't properly tell which direction it had come out of.

I struggled against the rope on my wrists as silently as I could. I didn't want to draw Hank back to me, not if I could help it.

Turning my head I caught sight of something against the wall. At first it looked like nothing more than a heap of bloodied clothes. It wasn't until a tiny whimper came from the pile that I realised it was human.

I focused harder, blinking the dirt and tears from my eyes. Her hair was usually blonde and curly but now it was matted to her head, blood and dirt making the colour almost impossible to distinguish. But I knew her face. Her blue eyes had dulled, the light that usually shone in them almost completely extinguished.

"Oh God, Kirsty."

I struggled harder against my bonds, the rope tightening as it dug into my flesh. At the mere mention of her name she seemed to whimper harder. I would have given anything in that moment to kill Hank. To reduce someone so sweet and innocent to this was beyond cruel.

"She's amazing, isn't she?"

Hank's voice sent bile racing up the back of my throat. I turned and watched as he stalked into the room and over to where Kirsty lay. She was too weak to even try and shuffle away from him and I watched as he almost lovingly pulled the blanket that lay over her away, exposing the horror that lay beneath.

Tears filled my eyes and I turned my head in time to throw up onto the floor next to me.

I'd thought I'd known a monster in Jude but Hank was something else.

"Don't look away, Heather, I want you to see what awaits you. I have so many plans for you. Kirsty here lasted much longer than I expected. I had thought after I finished working on her this morning that by the time I brought you home she'd be dead... But here she is still clinging to her pathetic life."

I closed my eyes in an attempt to block out what he was doing to her, the sadistic level of torture he was willing to inflict was beyond anything I was capable of dealing with.

"I suppose you want to help her, Heather, help stop her suffering?"

I didn't answer him holding myself perfectly still. I knew that if I opened my mouth I might start screaming and I might not be able to stop if I started.

"Aaron, wanted to help them too. He found out what I was doing to some of the people who were caught up in the operations... Walked in on me one night as I was elbow deep in a woman's abdomen, he didn't understand and she was a screamer. Stupid bitch wouldn't shut up and Aaron wasn't willing to wait for an explanation."

Hank fell silent for a moment. I opened my eyes as he shuffled across the floor towards me. His hands were covered in blood, Kirsty's blood.

"What I had to do to him… It's about the only thing I actually regret. I should have killed him then and there but for some reason…"

Hank trailed off, a faraway look filling his eyes.

"He couldn't remember what happened that night and I thought it didn't matter that I'd let him live. I thought we could continue on as we were but he left. And then when I found out afterwards that he was sent there to babysit me. The bastard pretended to be my friend…"

"You should have killed me that night."

Aaron's voice echoed through the room and I jerked against the rope that held me in place. I wanted to see him, part of me honestly believed that if I could just see him that all the horror I'd experienced would somehow be erased.

"I'd hoped it would take you a little longer to find me. I had planned to give you a gift… Little pieces of Heather, then we'd know how well you actually knew her, the assembly would require all your attention."

"You know this is between me and you, Hank, leave her out of it. If you want me, then come and get me."

The sound of something metal hitting the ground filled me with dread. I managed to strain around enough to catch sight of Aaron as he threw his gun on the floor.

"Aaron, no!"

I screamed at him as Hank stood a smile sliding across his face.

Hank streaked across the room, his speed surprising for a man of his size. The sound of their bodies colliding had me struggling against my bonds harder than ever. Something sharp bit into my skin as I dragged the rope over and back on it.

I felt it as it pierced my skin and still I didn't stop, my movements frantic as I struggled to get out of the bonds. They loosened enough for me to pull my hands free and I pushed up onto my feet.

Hank had Aaron on the floor, his hands wrapped around Aaron's throat. To me it looked as though he was physically trying to pull Aaron's head from his shoulders. I grabbed the first thing I laid eyes on, a metal bar that lay on the ground next to me.

I didn't think about what would happen as I ran at Hank and hoisted the bar over my head and brought it down across his shoulders. He slumped over Aaron, a growl of anger escaping him.

He turned, his hand reaching out for the bar in my hand. I fought against him but he was far stronger, he jerked me forward and sent me crashing back into the wall.

I slumped to the ground, darkness threatening to eat at my vision.

Aaron's face appeared above mine, his expression filled with concern as he gathered me into his arms.

"Heather, can you hear me?"

I groaned and tried to let the fog clear in my mind. I smiled up at Aaron, lifting my hand to his face as he scooped me up from the ground.

I started to open my mouth, my eyes darting past Aaron to find Hank. The other man pushed to his feet, the glint of a blade in his hand. I didn't get the opportunity to warn Aaron. The sound of a gun going off exploded in my ears. Hank jerked, once then twice as the bullets found their mark and he dropped to his knees.

I watched as the light slowly faded from his eyes, blood appearing on his lips before he fell face first down onto the dirty floor.

Footsteps thudded into the room in seconds the kitchen was filled with men in uniforms. The man holding the gun slowly approached Hank, the gun never wavering as he kept it trained on Hank's still form on the floor.

I watched as a uniformed officer crouched over Hank, he shook his head as he withdrew his hand from where he had checked for Hank's pulse.

"He's dead... It's finally over."

Aaron's whispered the words against my ear as he held me tighter. A fine tremor ran through him as he crushed my body to his chest.

Shouts and commands were issued and I watched my expression blank as the paramedics worked on Kirsty. The shock I felt over what had happened threatened to swallow me whole and it was a fight to hold it at bay. It would have been much easier to give into it but then I wouldn't know Aaron's touch.

"Are you alright?"

I nodded, "I just want to go home, hold Arianna in my arms and know that you're both safe."

I turned in Aaron's grip and wrapped my arms around him. Part of me had honestly believed that I would never have this again and yet I was still here... Despite what others had thrown at us, we were still together.

"Just take me home."

Aaron nodded and pressed his lips to the top of my head.

Chapter Nineteen

WEEKS PASSED BEFORE LIFE RETURNED to a sort of normalcy once more. There seemed to be a constant media presence, always wanting to know the truth of the situation with Hank and Jude, I truth I couldn't give them.

The only thing I was sure of was of my love for my family.

Standing in the french doors I stared out at Aaron as he played with Arianna. My heart swelled as I watched them together, my own perfect little unit.

Stepping out onto the wrap around porch I made my way over to them, Arianna's giggles filling me with a joy I hadn't ever believed I would get to experience.

Looking back on everything that had happened I knew I wouldn't change any of it, the terrible things Jude and

Hank had done to me had led to this moment and nothing would ever see me jeopardise it.

I held my hands out to Arianna as she waved her small clenched fists in the air.

"I think, Mommy, missed you."

Aaron smiled and whispered against Arianna's ear making her gurgle happily. She wrapped her tiny hands into his hair tugging it hard enough to make him wince.

"Where's David and Carrie?"

I asked as I sat down next to Aaron on the swing.

"House hunting, he wants somewhere before the baby gets here."

I nodded and grinned. Ever since Carrie had discovered she was pregnant David had changed even more. She was barely allowed to do anything anymore and he waited on her hand and foot. He would make a perfect father, much like his older brother.

"Gertrude wants to throw them a party when they find somewhere. I think she's finally starting to realise that if she doesn't change she's not going to play a part in the lives of her grandchildren."

Aaron's voice turned suddenly serious as he mentioned his mother. I reached over, wrapping my fingers through his.

"She's had a rough time…"

"But it doesn't give her the right to behave the way she did… She could have killed Carrie and…"

Aaron trailed off and shut his eyes. I knew the struggle he felt over his mother. He loved her and because of his father's betrayal I knew he wanted more than ever to draw her into the heart of the family. But I also knew until Gertrude changed that she wasn't someone Aaron would allow around his child.

Arianna settled in against Aaron's shoulder, her eyes drifting shut as he held her close. The dark circles that had sat beneath Aaron's eyes for a time after Hank's death were finally starting to fade and he was beginning to sleep at night. I knew he carried guilt over what had happened and I knew he blamed himself for what had happened to Kirsty. The only consolation in it all was that Hank hadn't killed her. Her physical wounds were beginning to heal but I had no idea how long it would take the emotional ones to reach a place where she could deal with them.

I watched as Aaron cradled our daughter, my own news bubbling within me. I'd wanted the perfect time to tell him, after everything that had happened I was hoping that Aaron would be pleased with what I had to tell him.

"You know how we were thinking about having more children in the future?"

I broached the topic slowly and carefully.

"Yeah."

He answered seemingly oblivious to what I was hinting at.

"What if the future was only eight and a half months away…"

Aaron shot me a confused look over Arianna's head.

"I don't understand?"

Reaching over to him I took his hand in mine and pressed it against my still flat stomach.

I watched as realisation dawned in his eyes.

"You mean you're?"

I nodded and smiled.

"I'm pregnant, I took the test a few days ago and I saw the doctor this morning, I wanted to be sure…"

Aaron drew me in against him, his eyes darkening with emotion.

"You beautiful perfect woman."

He whispered against my lips before kissing me softly.

The kiss didn't stay soft, it quickly deepened, Aaron's tongue sliding along my lips as he sought entry.

Arianna's grumble had him stop. She fussed and stirred in his arms and Aaron readjusted his hold on her.

"I think we'll have to wait until later for me to show you just how amazing I think you are."

A shiver of desire coursed over me as he cupped my cheek gently.

"I love you, Heather, you and Arianna and…"

His voice trailed off as he let his hand drop to my stomach.

"You're my world, I'd be nothing without you."

Smiling I pressed in against him, letting his arm wrap around my shoulders as he cradled me on the swing.

"I love you too, Aaron Ashcroft… Always and forever."

To find out more about this book or other in the
series, email M.G. Morgan
mille.g.morgan@gmail.com

Visit my website
http://milliemorganeroticromance.blogspot.com

Or join my mailing list for new release notices and
other little extras:
http://eepurl.com/rdBpP